It had been two years since she'd seen Roman Carter. Jackie's stomach knotted, and she kept her eyes as far away from him as possible.

She'd gotten to see enough in the first shocked moment when she figured out who he was. Dark hair, longish, falling into his face. A shadow of stubble on his strong chin, dimples when he'd smiled and the eyes, the familiar hazel eyes, self-assured, confident, cocky. He was the same Roman.

She could hear her father's angry voice in her mind. *He killed your brother. I will never forgive him. Never!*

She forced herself to take a breath. She had more important matters to worry about than Roman Carter. After he dropped her at the lodge she would put him out of her mind and push him back into the past where he belonged....

Books by Dana Mentink

Love Inspired Suspense

Killer Cargo
Flashover
Race to Rescue
Endless Night

DANA MENTINK

lives in California with her family. Dana and her husband met doing a dinner theater production of *The Velveteen Rabbit*. In college, she competed in national speech and debate tournaments. Besides writing novels, Dana taste-tests for the National Food Lab and freelances for a local newspaper. In addition to her work with Steeple Hill Books, she writes cozy mysteries for Barbour Books. Dana loves feedback from her readers. Contact her at www.danamentink.com.

Endless Night
Dana Mentink

Steeple
Hill®

Published by Steeple Hill Books™

STEEPLE HILL BOOKS

Steeple Hill®

Recycling programs
for this product may
not exist in your area.

ISBN-13: 978-0-373-44379-6

ENDLESS NIGHT

www.SteepleHill.com

Printed in U.S.A.

Come now, and let us reason together,
says the Lord,
Though your sins are as scarlet,
They will be as white as snow;
Though they are red like crimson,
They will be like wool.
—*Isaiah* 1:18

To my big sis, who has been there through all those dark nights that seemed endless.

ONE

She pressed down the fear. It was all a mistake, a terrible dream from which she'd awaken any moment. The crowded terminal of San Francisco International Airport was filled with people, talking on cell phones and checking flight information. In spite of the crowd, Jackie felt utterly alone as she stood in a corner near the busy ticket counters. Her phone rang. She jumped and clutched at it. "Hello?"

"Did you get a flight out?"

"Asia?" She hardly recognized her friend's voice. "I'm at the airport now but I've changed my mind. This is nuts. We can't run away. If Dr. Reynolds is guilty, we've got to stand our ground and prove it."

"Are you crazy?" Asia hissed. "You know Mick got jumped on his way over here after he called his friend in the police department. Reynolds has paid them off."

Jackie pressed the phone tightly to her ear. "There's got to be a mistake."

Asia's voice rose an octave. "Dr. Reynolds doesn't have the clout to buy off the police on his own. He's selling his patients' information to a crime ring. The errors are too widespread to be the work of one person. I should have seen it before."

Jackie tried to control her own panic. "We've both got to calm down. Where are you? Did you get Mick to a hospital?"

"I'm waiting for him at the clinic now. He's in a lot of pain. As soon as he can travel, we're gone." There was a sound of voices in the background. Asia spoke in a whisper. "You've got to get out of there, Jackie. Dr. Reynolds has men looking for us. They're trying to keep us quiet any way they can."

Jackie jerked around, scanning the crowd, and scooted into a farther corner.

Asia had been poring over the computer accounts in the darkened office, hours after closing time, downloading information to a thumb drive. Asia's boyfriend Mick who worked on the imaging equipment was there too, sipping coffee. Asia had just begun to explain why she'd summoned Jackie at such a late hour when Dr. Reynolds appeared, briefcase in hand. His wide forehead creased in suspicion.

"What are you three doing here? What are you downloading?"

Asia stood, facing him. "Dr. Reynolds, there are payments coming in for treatments we never provided. Addresses and personal information for our patients have been altered too."

The doctor's face purpled. "I've been watching you poking around, sticking your nose into things. What exactly are you saying?"

Mick stepped forward. "That you're guilty of fraudulent billing."

"It's more than that," Asia said, a tremor in her voice. "It's too widespread. You're working for somebody who does this on a large scale. "

Jackie watched in horror as Dr. Reynolds's face twisted in rage. "How dare you." Spittle flew from his mouth. "I'll ruin you. All of you." He spun around and ran from the room towards the back office.

At Asia's urging, Jackie had snatched the thumb drive and

crammed it in her pocket before Mick dragged both of the shocked women to the parking lot. "Go. Now. He keeps a gun in his office, I've seen it."

They raced to Jackie's car.

Mick kissed Asia. "Go to the coffee shop. Wait for my call."

Asia's eyes filled. "Where are you going?"

"I have a friend at the S.F. P.D. I'm going to contact him. I'll meet you. It will be okay."

But it wasn't. He'd returned bloodied and battered.

"I was jumped. They wore masks but I recognized one. He's a cop. Reynolds must have bought them off."

Asia had taken Mick to the nearest clinic, promising to meet Jackie at the airport.

"Listen, I've been keeping detailed notes on all the inconsistencies I've found." Asia started to talk faster. "I contacted someone who used to work for Dr. Reynolds at his office in Thousand Oaks. She's looking too. You've got to give me and Mick some time. We'll call you as soon as we can. Just get away somewhere, anywhere." The phone disconnected.

Jackie's breath seemed to form hard crystals in her lungs. Mick beaten? Dirty cops? Crime rings? The whole thing was absurd. She quickly dialed her friend Patti's cell number.

"Hey, Jackie. You're out of milk. I came to borrow some before rehearsal. I should have taken up a smaller instrument. I work up an awful thirst dragging that cello up five flights."

"Patti, listen. I've got to go out of town. Can you take care of the place?"

"Sure, where you going?"

"Just a quick getaway."

"Sounds great. You know I'm kinda miffed. You never mentioned your darling boyfriend."

She felt a stir of alarm. "That's because I don't have one."

"Care to explain the good-looking cop who stopped by? He was in plainclothes, of course, but he showed me a badge."

Jackie froze, unable to speak.

Patti continued. "Handsome fella. How can you resist an ex-Navy man? Just the thought of dating a sailor gives me a charge."

"I don't…."

"He told me that you decided to break things off because of his dangerous job and all that. He wanted to come patch things up. He wondered if you'd left town, maybe gone to Maryland."

"Maryland?" The lights flickered before her eyes. *He knows I have family in Maryland?* Jackie forced a cheerful tone. "He sure has put a lot of thought into it, hasn't he?"

"I guess so. Anyway, I gotta go."

"Can you take care of my things until I get back?"

"Okay, but you're going to have an empty fridge by that time. Bye."

Jackie squeezed the phone between her clammy palms.

The stranger knew her father was in Maryland. He knew where she lived here in San Francisco. The cop, if he really was a cop, was probably out right now checking all the places she frequented. Dr. Reynolds had set things in motion with alarming speed. She could feel nothing but cold, blind panic.

An image of Roman rose in her mind, the rock solid strength that had never failed her except for the one awful moment in Alaska that had changed everything. She thought of his laughter and sense of adventure, which had been a balm for her as long as she could remember. *That part of your life is dead, Jackie.* She blinked the memory back into the past where it belonged.

In a fog she joined the end of the nearest ticket line. For the first time, she considered where she could go. She just needed time, time to think things through, a safe place to figure out a plan. Not in Maryland—she could never risk involving her father. He'd be safe as long as she stayed far away until things were settled.

The line snaked its way along until Jackie found herself at the front. The efficient woman behind the desk looked at her. "Where to?"

"I…" Speech failed her. What place would be safe until she could climb out of the mess she'd gotten herself into?

"What is your destination, ma'am?"

She would fly to the farthest corner she could think of, the place that held her most precious memories and the echoes of her most terrible nightmare. Jackie's mouth formed the word, but her mind did not believe it.

"Alaska."

Roman Carter drove the rattletrap van with Wayne's Aviation emblazoned on the side to the small airport on the edge of town. The day was clear, the roads newly plowed of snow. He felt an unusual surge of optimism. Maybe the tourists would start to come again, in spite of the economy. If the flight load picked up, he might be able to make progress toward owning his own plane.

He pulled up at the airstrip that cut its way through the tiny town of Foster and headed toward the two people in the shuttle-waiting area, a heavyset, dark-haired man with a mustache, and a small figure, bundled into a coat that wasn't warm enough with a crumpled baseball hat pulled down low over the brim.

"Hello, folks. I understand you need a ride to the Delucchi Lodge."

The heavyset man nodded and extended a hand. "Byron Lloyd."

"Roman Carter. Good to meet you." Roman noticed a price tag sticking out from the neck of the man's jacket and hid a smile.

The man followed Roman's look and detached the price tag with a chuckle. "Luggage got lost somewhere. All I have is my duffel bag—it's a good thing I carry it everywhere. Had to buy this jacket at the airport, and it cost me a good chunk of change."

Roman turned to the other figure, wondering at first if the person was hard of hearing. After a long moment, she lifted her chin so he got a good view of her face.

"We've already met," she said.

He blinked in shock. Jackie Swann stood before him, strands of her copper hair trailing from underneath her hat, amber eyes looking at him with a mixture of surprise and anger. He couldn't speak.

Jackie cleared her throat and straightened her small frame. "I didn't know you worked for the Delucchis."

He forced his mouth to start moving. "I don't. I work for Wayne Fisk. I fly people to the lodge." The fierce desire to ask why she was here burned in him. *Why would she come back?* He bit down on the words, forcibly stilling the barrage of feelings that whipped through him like a savage Alaskan storm. He moved to take her small bag.

She grabbed it before he could. "I'll carry it."

"Fine." The two followed him out to the shuttle. Byron Lloyd filled the strained silence by peppering Roman with questions.

"I'm a freelance writer, you see. Covering this Winterfest deal. A festival to celebrate winter. Clever marketing. How many people are you expecting?"

"Hard to say. Not as many travelers these days."

"Am I going to get cell phone coverage and Internet at the lodge?"

"Internet, yes. No cell unless you have a satellite phone."

They arrived at the airstrip and loaded the plane. Roman hated to do it, but he asked Jackie to sit in the front to balance the weight properly. She reluctantly agreed. He offered an arm as she climbed up into the plane, but she ignored it.

He ducked into the office to check in with Wayne once more before he flew out.

Wayne looked up from his top-of-the-line computer and

gave Roman a close look. "What's the matter? You look like you've seen a ghost."

"It's nothing." He walked to the plane feeling that Wayne was right. The ghost of his past, of his sins, of his longings, had come back to dredge up the horror he'd tried so hard to put behind him. Looking at Jackie's delicate profile as she stared out the window, he wondered.

Why are you here?

TWO

Jackie stared out the window at the blinding white below. She felt it inside too—a stark, flat feeling, as though her heart was as frozen and untouchable as the tundra. Why hadn't she seen it coming? Roman had always been interested in flying. He loved the outdoors. It was a logical leap that he would still be working in Alaska, but she never suspected he would be so closely connected to Delucchi Lodge. Not after what had happened, not after two long years.

Her stomach knotted and she kept her gaze as far away from Roman as possible. Dark hair, longish, falling into his face. A shadow of stubble on his strong chin, dimples when he'd smiled at Byron Lloyd, and the eyes, the familiar hazel eyes, self-assured, confident, cocky. In the two years they'd been apart, nothing had changed. He was the same Roman.

She could hear her father's angry voice in her mind.

He killed your brother. I will never forgive him. Never.

They had had only one tortured conversation after the accident. It was the only time she'd seen Roman completely vulnerable, unable to even form a coherent sentence, his then twenty-three-year-old face twisted in agony. She closed her eyes at the awful memory.

Squeezing her hands together she forced herself to take a

breath. She had more important matters to worry about than Roman. After he dropped her at the lodge she would put him out of her mind.

At the airport in San Francisco, she'd bought a satellite phone, though she'd almost choked at the thousand-dollar price tag. She had to be sure Asia could reach her, so she e-mailed her the phone number via her laptop just before the flight. It might be a risk if Reynolds's people could hack into her e-mail, so she sent only the phone number and didn't include any other details. She wished again that Asia and Asia's boyfriend, Mick, had come along. But Asia was right—Mick needed medical attention for his injuries and it was probably smarter for them not to fly together, anyway. In the agonizing hours before the plane departed, she'd been lucky enough to find a place in the airport to charge her phone and to buy a duffel bag and some sundries. There were no messages from her friend through the Internet or on her home answering machine. Where was she? Jackie could still hear the panic in her friend's voice.

Just get away somewhere, anywhere.

Under the pretense of studying the mountains, she shot a glance behind her at Byron Lloyd. She found him gazing at her intently.

"Where do you hail from?" he asked.

Jackie's stomach knotted. "West Coast."

"Whereabouts?"

She forced a smile. "Oh, you know. Here and there. How about you?"

"San Francisco area."

Her gut twisted even further. "Well, you'll love the Delucchi Lodge." She realized she'd given herself away.

"Oh, you've been there before?"

She nodded, saved from a reply when Roman took the plane down toward the cleared strip of frozen ground. She saw Skip

Delucchi waiting, his hair a little sparser than she remembered, his long face and prominent nose giving him a hound-dog look.

Skip wrapped her in a hug when she dropped down from the plane. "Jackie, it's so good to see you. I was completely surprised when you called me from the airport. Thank goodness we had one cabin still vacant." He shot an uneasy glance at Roman, who was pulling luggage out of the plane's cargo hold. He lowered his voice. "Did you and Roman get a chance to catch up?"

"No. I'm not feeling chatty, I guess."

He hesitated for a moment. "Yes, well, it doesn't matter. June is so excited that you're here. She hasn't stopped baking since sunup."

Skip introduced himself to Lloyd, who Jackie noticed had been taking in their conversation with interest. He helped them into a battered Range Rover and, with a final word to Roman, headed toward the distant lights of the lodge. Jackie glanced quickly into the side mirror. Roman stood tall and straight against an unforgiving glare of white. In the distance, above the snow-crusted bluff, she thought she could just make out the roofline of the still unfinished cabin, the place where everything had ended in the blink of an eye.

In spite of the circumstances, the sight of the Delucchi Lodge stirred a warm nostalgia in her. She savored the profile of the rugged mountains that backed the property and the thick stand of snow-topped pines that stood sentry around the main cabin. Smaller cabins were sprinkled along the property. A massive set of antlers festooned the doorway, and Jackie was greeted by the smell of roasting meat and apple pie.

June appeared in the tiled hallway, wiping her hands on a worn apron. Her dishwater-blond hair hung in a careless chop at her shoulders, her blue eyes accented by deep crow's feet that Jackie had not noticed two years before.

"You look wonderful. I'm so glad you're here." She wrapped

Jackie in a cinnamon-scented embrace. "Fallon will be glad too. I wonder where she is, anyway."

Jackie was not so sure about Fallon's reception. Fallon had only wanted to be around Jackie because of her brother. The girl had adored Danny with the deep passion of a love-struck teenager.

They exchanged more pleasantries until Skip offered to show Jackie and Byron to their cabins. "Be dark in a couple hours. Best get you settled in." He turned to Jackie. "You're staying in Riverrun. I thought you'd like that."

Jackie nodded. "That's perfect. I'll go myself. You take care of Mr. Lloyd." Jackie thanked him and watched the two march off into the snow. She was dismayed to discover when they stopped that Lloyd would have the cabin closest to hers. *Just relax, Jackie. He's a nosy reporter, that's all.*

She was about to head out herself when June stopped her. "Jackie, what were you thinking, coming here with that flimsy jacket? Did you forget we're north of the Arctic Circle?" She fetched a heavy coat from the closet and helped her into it.

Making her way to her cabin, Jackie wondered if her abrupt arrival had inconvenienced Skip and June. Perhaps she should turn around and leave. But it was not the time to make such decisions so late in the day, not in Alaska, not this time of year when there was only a scant four hours of sunlight each day. She resolved to at least help June in the kitchen and ease any burdens she might have caused by showing up on short notice.

As she turned around to pick up her duffel, she saw Lloyd looking out his small cabin window, his dark eyes fixed on her. The curtain quickly fell into place as he stepped back out of sight.

With a surge of fear, she closed her cabin door.

Roman flew the plane past trees thoroughly crusted with ice, against the backdrop of rigid mountains. He was relieved to take off, glad to be alone with his thoughts.

The shock of seeing Jackie still tingled in every nerve. She looked different than the last time he'd seen her, the grief not as fresh in her face. An anger had taken its place and rooted itself deeply in her eyes.

The guilt swirled up like wind-whipped snow. Jackie still despised him, and he despised himself for what had happened those two years ago.

He tried to concentrate on the feeling of the plane as it banked smoothly. He had to remind himself that the beautiful de Havilland did not belong to him and never would, unless business picked up. He'd been saving every dime he made, but he was still fifty thousand dollars short. Fifty thousand roadblocks separated him and his dream, the only dream he had left.

He was admiring the spectacular dazzle of snow on the gray mountains, highlighted by the sun on its way to setting, when the radio crackled.

"Roman, June needs your help. Fallon's gone. June's half-frantic," Wayne said.

Roman sighed. "Where'd she head this time?"

"Her mom isn't sure. Went out to do some cross-country skiing."

"By herself?" Roman checked his watch. Almost one-thirty. The sun would set in a little under an hour.

"She told her mom she was meeting friends, but all of them are home safe and sound where they belong. Skip is out right now on the snowmobile looking for her."

"Give me her last location and I'll check it out."

Wayne filled him in. "Don't stay out too long. There's a low pressure building over the Gulf. We're gonna get some snow."

With a sense of rising urgency, he banked and turned the plane. It wasn't a game this far north. If you got lost in the great white expanse you might survive, in the daytime. If you got lost in the dark, when temperatures plunged deep into the minus range, that was a whole other can of worms. Wayne had taught him early on to carry a survival kit. No exceptions. Picturing the stubborn, careless sixteen-year-old Fallon, he knew she hadn't taken any such precautions.

Fallon was hard to like, harder to trust, and he should be mad about having to go bail her out. Instead he only felt the same lancing pain when he thought of the younger Fallon, barely a teen with a puppy-love crush on Danny, who loved her as if she were his own sister. He blinked away the image of Jackie that rose again in his thoughts, the strange mixture of pleasure and pain that her presence awakened in him. What was she doing at this very moment? Asleep in her cabin? Knowing her, she was probably out helping to look for Fallon.

He peered closer at the darkening ground. The sun was low on the horizon, painting the snow in silver and gray. Fallon would have worn the old green jacket she practically lived in, so he strained his eyes to see any flash of the color.

The temperature continued to drop steadily. A paltry three degrees Fahrenheit began to slide into the negative numbers. Wind vibrated the wings of the plane and rose along with Roman's anxiety.

Darkness spread. Soon it would be difficult to land safely.

Wayne radioed him again. "Come back in now."

"A few more minutes."

"Now, Roman. Plenty of rescuers die trying to be the hero. Don't be one of them."

He got a glimpse of the unfinished cabin on the bluff and fought a shudder. "I know. I'll be careful."

"That's not good enough." Wayne's voice became commanding.

Roman thought of Danny, foggy images of that dark, frigid night swirling up again, the frightening sounds of the car sliding over the embankment clear in his ears. No one else would die in this wintry abyss if he could help it, especially no one whom Danny had loved. "Sorry, Wayne." Roman turned the radio down to mute Wayne's anxious retort. "There's no way I can turn my back now."

He fought against the wind that buffeted the plane in the near darkness. At this latitude, night did not come gently. It arrived like a heavy fist-fall in a matter of minutes. Soon there would be no chance of finding her.

"Come on, Fallon. Where are you?"

As if on cue he caught sight of a green flash under the massive trunk of a pine. He immediately scanned the surface for the best place to land. There was no time to go through the tedious safety checks he'd done before. He had to put the plane down quickly. Praying he would not land in an overflow that would plunge him into water or freeze the skis so completely they would stay riveted there until the spring thaw, he took it down.

Engines still running, he jumped out, the snow against his legs taking his breath away. He hurried over to find Fallon, back against the tree, arms folded.

"Are you okay?"

She turned her long, thin face in his direction. "Yeah."

"Yeah? That's it? Your dad has been searching for you. What are you doing out here?"

She huffed. "Don't give me a lecture. I wanted to cross-country, but one of my skis broke, so I quit. I figured someone would come along and here you are."

He bit back the frustration and found his satellite phone. Skip Delucchi picked up on the first ring.

"Did you find her?"

"Yes, she's fine." Roman gave him the location.

"Can you fly her out?"

Roman looked at the sky. "No. I'm grounded for the night."

Skip let out a long sigh. "Jackie and I are about a mile from there on the snowmobile. We're having a little trouble with one of the vehicles, but we'll be there soon."

Jackie. He caught himself before he said the name aloud. He'd been right about her joining in the search. Roman clicked off the phone and turned to Fallon. "Why don't you get in the plane and warm up?"

Fallon's face still wore a sullen cast, but she climbed aboard. Roman joined her and they sat in silence watching the sun disappear behind the horizon.

Fallon's voice startled him. "Why is she here?"

"Who?" he asked, though he knew exactly whom she referred to.

"You know. I heard Dad talking to her on the phone."

He felt her staring at him in the gloom. He wanted to deny it, to steer the conversation elsewhere, but he couldn't lie to the girl. "I'm not sure."

Fallon folded her arms across her chest. "I didn't think she'd ever come back. I wouldn't, if I got out of here."

He felt the rise of pain again, but didn't answer.

"So she hates you."

He nodded. "Pretty much."

"That's heavy."

Almost heavier than he could bear sometimes. He was saved from further questions by Skip's arrival on the snowmobile, headlights blazing through the gloom. Jackie pulled up a moment after him. Swallowing his emotion, Roman helped Fallon down and Skip enfolded her in a hug. She remained stiff in his arms, but Roman thought he could see tenderness on her face, a sliver of the innocent child she had been. Jackie stood apart.

What was she thinking? He wondered again why she had come back to a place that obviously held such pain for her, for them both.

Skip shook Roman's hand vigorously and hugged him. "How can I thank you?"

"A hot meal sometime would do it."

"You are welcome at our table any day. June has all kinds of savories and sweets in the works for Winterfest." He smiled at Jackie. "Can you put Roman on your machine?"

Roman didn't wait to see the uncomfortable look on her face. "No need. I'm staying with the plane."

Skip blinked. "You'll freeze out here."

"I've got gear. I'll radio Wayne and let him know."

Skip shook his head. "I don't think so. We're going to get snow tonight. It's too dangerous."

Jackie continued to look at him with expressionless eyes. "You can ride with me if you need to."

The offer was kind but the tone was not. It was just as cold as the breathtakingly icy air around them. "I appreciate your concern, but this bird is my responsibility and I'm not leaving her. I'm prepared. I'll survive until morning and I've got a radio and sat phone if I need to bail out. I'm staying."

With a sigh, Skip shook his hand once more and helped Fallon onto his snowmobile. Jackie followed Skip without a backward glance. She tried to start her snowmobile but the engine would not turn over. After several minutes of useless trying from all of them, Skip put his hands on his hips. "Well, I'll have to make two trips." He shot a glance from Jackie to Roman. "Jackie, can you stay here while I take Fallon back, and then I'll come for you?"

Jackie looked as though she'd been sentenced to prison. Roman saw her take a breath before she answered. "Of course."

Skip and Fallon headed off into the dark.

Roman cleared his throat. "Let's sit in the plane. Warmer there."

He thought she would refuse, but the steadily dropping temperature must have convinced her because she climbed in the passenger-side door. They sat for a moment in silence before she spoke, her voice oddly flat.

"This place hasn't changed at all. It looks exactly the same as the first time I saw it. I was just a college kid. Danny was a freshman in high school."

He nodded. "No, not really. Still plenty of wide open spaces." But it had changed, profoundly. The woman who used to be the center of his world, the first thing he thought of every morning and the last thing before sleep claimed him at night could barely look at him. Fixed in his mind was the time when Jackie's father, an engineer on the pipeline, had brought his family to spend nearly the entire year in Alaska. Each season he'd shown Jackie the wonders of this isolated place, and each day had brought them closer together.

He remembered when they had built a series of snow igloos and invited all their friends to camp out under the stars. Was it his imagination or had the stars now lost some of their luster? He felt Jackie's eyes on him and shifted. "Just thinking about our snow igloos. Remember that?"

For a moment, the spark shone in her eyes again, a smile lit her face that took his breath away. Then it disappeared. "I remember." Her tone was so low he almost didn't catch it. "I remember. Danny talked about it all the time."

"Yeah." He wanted to take her hands in his, to tell her again how deeply sorry he was. He knew she could never love him again, but he wanted desperately to bring back to life the warm and ebullient woman she had been, the woman who sang Broadway show tunes at every opportunity and cried at the sight of an injured animal. "Jackie, I…" Words failed him.

She looked at him, waiting for him to finish. When he didn't, she let out a little sigh and steered them back onto safe ground. "I forgot how dark it gets here."

"Sure does."

She shivered and he offered her a blanket. She took it and he helped her tuck it in around her shoulders, his fingers tingling where they accidentally brushed against hers. She started to say something, then stopped. They sank into heavy silence.

The distance that grew between them in that moment might have been wider than the sprawling Alaskan wilderness. A twist of pain lanced through him as he recalled bittersweet memories.

Oddly it was a moment in San Francisco that crystallized his future in Alaska. He'd had to content himself with Jackie's periodic visits, until her father had a stroke that left him unable to travel. Roman had hoarded every last penny and flown to San Francisco to see her that year. On one fog-shrouded night, she'd said the words that made him sure their lives would be intertwined forever. "I feel like Alaska is my real home," she'd said. That's when he'd decided to ask her to marry him as soon as her father was well. He'd flown home and begun counting the days until her return.

Thinking about the joy he'd felt numbed him inside

It seemed like an eternity before Skip appeared to retrieve Jackie and they motored across the snow. When the sound of the snowmobile engine died away, Roman radioed Wayne and calmly accepted a vigorous tongue-lashing.

Before he bunked in for the night, Roman ventured once more into the ink-dark night. The sight never failed to take his breath away. A cathedral of achingly brilliant stars shone between the clouds without the interference of city lights. He felt as if he could reach up and touch one of the dazzling gems.

Wish on a star, his mother had told him when he was a boy.

As the cold closed in around him he knew that there was no point in childish wishing. What his heart had once desired might as well be as far away as those perfect stars. Worst of all, he was grateful for the distance.

THREE

Jackie's mind raced as she and Skip headed back to the lodge. She fought against shivers that had started the moment she had sat next to Roman in that cockpit. His nearness had unnerved her. She flashed back to her impulsive brother, riding off a snowy ridge and cracking his collarbone. He'd had his arm in a sling just before the accident that had taken his life. Ironic that it had been Roman at the wheel that night, not her reckless brother. *Remember that, Jackie.* She swallowed hard as Skip parked the snowmobile and they made their way toward the comfortable living room of the Delucchi Lodge.

Fallon sat on a couch, still wearing her jacket. Jackie could tell by the stiff set of her shoulders that the girl was upset. Jackie remembered Fallon as a moody teen, smitten with her handsome brother, but hadn't there been something else? At the end, before Jackie's brother died, there had been some anger, some unusual explosiveness in the girl. At the time, she'd attributed it to teen angst, but now as she looked at her, she wondered if she had missed something.

"Oh, sweetie," June said, entering the room. She smiled at Jackie before catching her daughter's hands. "I still can't believe you were out there all alone. That gives me goose bumps."

Fallon pulled her hands away. "I've already told you I'm fine, Mom. You don't have to get all crazy about it again."

June shot Jackie a rueful look and left when a timer sounded in the kitchen.

After repelling any attempts at conversation, Fallon sat on the couch, water droplets sparkling on her straight brown hair. She kept her gaze fastened to the window. Sounds of June washing dishes floated into the cozy space over the crackle of a fire in the old stone hearth. In the adjoining room, a newly married couple sipped from mugs as they cuddled together on a love seat with reindeer-horn armrests. Skip was tending to the snowmobiles and somewhere, out in the endless night, was Roman.

Roman. Even his name brought to life a storm of emotion inside her. It was no longer the feeling she'd nursed since she was a teen, the all-consuming love for him that grew every time she came to stay. Now it had changed into something else, twisted by anger, misshapen by grief, but still with an undercurrent of longing that she could not explain. With a sigh, she rose to warm her hands by the fire.

Fallon's voice startled her. "Was your dad here when they built this place?"

"The lodge? No. Why do you ask?"

"I just wondered who helped, is all. I heard they hired some people who were in town for the summer to build the cabins. Gave them room and board and some stayed on awhile after to be on staff here. I wasn't born then."

Jackie looked at her quizzically. "I'm sure they did. When we came the first time, it was just your parents and a housekeeper, Dax and another man, I think."

The girl's eyes seemed to blaze with reflected firelight. "So why did you come back now?"

Jackie kept her tone light. "I needed to get away."

"From what?"

She looked at the fire. "Things at work were stressful. I wanted a change of scenery."

"That's weird."

"What?"

"That you'd come back here, after two years. To the place where Danny died. And seeing Roman and all. That must be weird, too."

Jackie swallowed. *You have no idea.* Weirdest of all was the way she couldn't seem to get Roman out of her mind. His face, his voice, the golden green of his eyes. "I didn't know he'd be here. I figured he'd left to join the air force, like he'd always talked about."

"I guess people don't always do what you think they will."

Jackie turned to face her, trying to read the expression in the girl's face. "Is something wrong, Fallon?"

She chewed at a fingernail. "No."

She intended to press her further when Skip came in, eyeing them nervously.

"Getting reacquainted?" He sat down next to his daughter. "You really had us concerned there, kitten."

Fallon turned her face away. "I can take care of myself."

"Sure you can. We just worry, that's all. Alaska's a pretty big place."

"Not big enough," Fallon muttered before jumping off the sofa and leaving the room.

Skip gave Jackie a tired smile. "And I thought the hard part was when she was a toddler, sticking her fingers in light sockets. That was a walk in the park compared to this teen thing."

June reappeared with steaming mugs of cocoa and Byron Lloyd at her elbow.

"Daughter okay?" Lloyd asked, his full cheeks pink over the collar of his jacket.

"Yes, she's fine," Skip said. "How did you know she was missing?"

He chuckled and pointed to Jackie. "Heard people calling her name. Saw this young lady scurry off and heard the snowmobile engines. Saw Mrs. Delucchi all worried. I put two and two together."

Jackie looked at him closely. He'd been watching her, all right—following her every move.

He stared back at her. "You look pretty comfortable on a snowmobile. Must have put in some time on one when you visited here before."

"Some," she said. "You know, I'm really tired. Jet-lagged. I think I'll go back to my cabin now."

Skip hugged her, and Lloyd offered a cheerful wave as she left.

The frigid air grabbed her in an icy fist as she walked into the darkness. Living in California had stripped her of her cold-weather hardiness. Danny would have laughed. He'd always been impervious to the cold. She looked up into the brilliant sky, decorated with a breathtaking swath of stars and felt suddenly very small and very alone.

Had Reynolds' men figured out she'd run? Had Asia and Mick found a place to hide? Terror balled up in her stomach, and it took all her willpower to suppress it.

With a deep weariness, she unlocked the door to her small cabin and went inside. The woven throw rug and exposed pine beams of the ceiling should have made her feel cozy and secure, but she could not shake the inner chill. She lit a small fire, prepared a steaming cup of tea and sat down in a sturdy, hand-carved chair to put her thoughts in order.

Coming to Alaska had been a huge mistake. It made her question her other recent decisions. Maybe the entire situation with her boss was one big misunderstanding. Dr. Reynolds was a respected cardiologist, yet Asia had stumbled onto evidence that he was selling patient information, possibly to a crime ring, which then submitted fraudulent claims through a vast network of companies.

Maybe they should have gone to the cops. Even if Dr. Reynolds and his network had paid off some of them, he couldn't have the whole police department under their thumb.

She thought again about the cop who'd shown up at her apartment. He'd known all about her. Had he learned all about her friends too? A tremor swept through her body. Had Mick and Asia found refuge somewhere? She dialed the phone to check messages on her voice mail. There was only one. The voice was low and raspy. But the words were clear as ice.

If you tell anyone what happened, your father will pay.

Panic set in, filling her up until she thought she would scream. The only thing that kept her from bolting straight to the airport was Asia. She had to know Mick and Asia were okay before she ran again. E-mail. Maybe Asia had sent a message.

Jackie reached out with trembling hands to boot up her laptop, when her heart thudded to a stop. Was it her imagination? Perhaps her hands were hot from the tea. She felt the top of the machine again. There was a faint trace of heat there, as if it had been turned on recently.

In spite of the warmth, her body went dead cold. Somebody was spying on her.

Roman inhaled the frigid air as if it could somehow freeze away the thoughts that tormented him. The faint scent of Jackie lingered on the blanket, a clean fragrance of soap that toyed with his heart. He pressed it to his nose and inhaled deeply. Though the comforting hum of a generator kept the heater going, the minus-fifteen-degree temperature forced its way in. Sitting in the plane, a sleeping bag wrapped around his shoulders, he studied the way the moonlight bathed the frozen ground in luminous silver. It could be so beautiful and so deadly.

Still, winter held so many fabulous memories, framed by snowy days spent with Jackie. Each winter brought her back, more beautiful and full of life than the previous one. Had it really been only two years since he'd decided to propose to her? He'd saved every dime for the Tlingit ring, an intricate twist of gold and silver, the twining together of the eagle and raven.

Then all his dreams came to a halt in one horrific moment. He felt the cold inside now, and it had nothing to do with the air. If he'd just said no to Danny's request for a ride into town. If he'd only seen the unstable layers in the snowpack that would sweep them off the road. The stubborn part of his conscience spoke again. *There was something else, something on that night that shouldn't have been there.* He could not pull the detail out of his foggy memory any more now that he could two years ago. The amnesia had not diminished.

"Doesn't matter anyway. I was behind the wheel. I killed him and I'll have to live with that forever," he whispered, his breath condensing in the air. He hadn't asked God for forgiveness, because deep down he knew he did not deserve it. He should pay, and had been paying for the last two years, going on a lifetime. He'd somehow survived without the love that had been the biggest part of his life, and he'd thought those feelings would remain buried forever. He'd believed it, until she'd come back.

The radio crackled to life.

"You're a hardheaded fool," Wayne Fisk boomed.

Roman couldn't resist a smile. "Yeah, I know, but you're going to get this bird back in one piece."

"As long as the pilot doesn't wind up freezing to death or getting chewed by bears."

"No bear would eat me."

"True. Not enough fat to savor, all muscle and gristle."

Roman laughed.

After a pause, Wayne continued. "It's really something that Jackie's back."

"Uh-huh. How come you didn't warn me? You had to have seen her name when she booked?"

"That's the funny thing. She used the name J. Marley, so I didn't connect it. Didn't figure it out at all until June told me a minute ago, when she called to make the next set of flight arrangements for the guests."

Marley. Her mother's maiden name. Roman realized Wayne had fallen uncharacteristically silent. "Still there?"

"Sure. I just wondered how you're doing, since she's back."

"I'm fine."

"Thought it might be uncomfortable being so close."

He spoke more loudly than he'd intended. "We aren't going to be close. I'm sure we won't even see each other while she's staying here."

"Not unless you want to."

Roman shifted uneasily. "Thanks for checking in. I'll see you as soon as I can thaw her out tomorrow."

"Right. Stay warm."

"Roger that." As he turned off the radio, a movement in the tree line caught his attention.

So what was Jackie doing here now? Under a different name? Clearly she hadn't planned the trip, showing up in an inadequate jacket with only a duffel bag in hand. And there was something in her eyes, besides the anger and pain. There was a shade of fear. The thought of her being afraid made his breath come up short. Was she in some sort of trouble?

He knew she did not want his help and he would never be able to offer it. Still, it wouldn't hurt to keep an eye on things.

As long as he did it from a distance.

FOUR

Jackie floated briefly into wakefulness the next morning to the sound of a plane flying over. She knew it was Roman, on his way to pick up supplies or people at the airport. Part of her felt relieved that he had made it through the unforgiving Alaskan night intact. No one else should lose their lives at this beautiful lodge, even someone she never wanted to see again. She drifted back into another hour of fitful sleep, awaking groggy and dazed.

She lay for a moment, pretending she was on vacation. The fantasy didn't last long. The threat from her voicemail chilled her. She wrapped herself in her jacket, having left her robe in San Francisco, and checked her phone for messages, calling back to her apartment to check there, too. Nothing. Her stomach knotted into a tight ball. Next she booted up the laptop and sat, foot tapping, urging the machine to work faster.

It finally loaded the messages and she found what she was looking for. Asia had sent a brief message in the late hours of the previous night.

Be at Delucchi's soon. Mick is well enough to travel. Got to resolve this before it's too late. When Mick worked at his brother's practice they had a similar problem. One doctor lost his license for fraudulent billing. Cops thought

he was working with a crime ring but never had enough to convict him. Gotta have an airtight case. I'm onto a new lead. We'll talk soon.
Asia

She was so happy to hear from her friend, the implication didn't hit her at first. Be at Delucchi's soon? How had Asia found her? Jackie's pulse pounded.

Her fingers hammered out a frantic message, hoping her friend was online, praying no one was hacking into their e-mails.

Are you okay? Location?

When no return e-mail arrived she thought about the thumb drive tucked in her bag. Buried somewhere in the data it contained was enough evidence to incriminate the crime ring and Reynolds. It also had plenty of confidential patient information on it. Second, now Jackie was definitely in deep, possessing information she had no right to.

Uncertainty surged through her again. What should she do? Was it safe for Asia to come, with Lloyd watching every move and the threat left on her voicemail? She typed quickly.

Might be trouble here. Don't come.

She'd just hit the send button when a knock at the door made her jump. She hurriedly closed the file and shut the laptop screen before she went to the door.

Byron Lloyd stood there, bundled in a ski jacket, scarf and hat, stamping up and down to keep warm. "Morning." His voice thundered through the small cabin. "Heading in for breakfast. Figured you might want an escort."

He looked past her. "Are you working? Thought you were on vacation."

"I am. I'm not quite ready for breakfast. I'll be there in a few minutes. You go on without me."

"You sure?"

She nodded. "Quite sure. Go on ahead, please."

He gave her a jolly smile and headed out, crunching across the newly fallen snow, through the still-dark morning. She watched until he'd entered the lodge and pulled the drapes more firmly closed. She put the thumb drive in her pocket and deleted the e-mail. If Lloyd, or anybody else, came snooping around, they wouldn't find incriminating documents on her computer. She pulled on the warmest clothes she'd brought and pocketed the thumb drive. Pulling her hair into a ponytail, she surveyed the damage of a sleepless night. Shadows under her eyes, freckles standing out in sharp contrast to her pale skin. Sighing, she slicked on some sunscreen and carefully locked the cabin door behind her as she left.

The moonlight shone on the large footprints Lloyd had left as she approached the lodge. What had he said on the plane ride from the airport? She'd been so overwhelmed at seeing Roman she hadn't listened fully. He was a reporter, covering the Winterfest events for a paper? Magazine? Which one? Had he mentioned a name? She made a decision to find out. Lloyd wasn't the only one who could ask nosy questions. It made her feel marginally better to go on the offensive, at least with Lloyd.

She could just make out people busy filling front loaders with snow and emptying them into huge wooden boxes in front of the lodge, where the land flattened out for several acres. It clicked in her mind. The snow sculpture competitions would start the next day. Each participant got his or her precisely measured square of compacted snow to fashion a fantastic frozen work of art. She'd watched the competition many years running, always in awe of the talented artists who showed up to win the thousand-dollar prize. Skip had lobbied hard for years to host the competition and he'd finally been successful.

A person loaded up with a stack of boxes approached the lodge. Jackie scooted ahead to hold the door. The figure hesitated for a moment. Jackie shivered when she recognized the man.

"Thanks," Roman said. "June's cooking supplies."

"You're welcome." Jackie noticed he seemed thinner than she remembered, but his arms and broad shoulders seemed just as iron-strong as he hefted the heavy crates with ease over the threshold. He disappeared down the hallway and she joined the assorted diners in the family eating-area. A huge fire was crackling and the room was filled with cheerful laughter and conversation. She recognized the honeymooning couple, a portly man and his wife, with skin nearly as white as their matching sweaters, and Byron Lloyd. Purposefully sliding into the empty space next to Lloyd, she filled her plate with scrambled eggs, June's homemade blueberry scones and succulent sausages.

Her stomach growled and it dawned on Jackie that she hadn't eaten a full meal since before her flight. She tried not to wolf down the food.

"Did you sleep well, Mr. Lloyd?"

"Like a log. I've been traveling for work for the past twenty-five years so I can pretty much sleep on anything. You?"

"Fairly well. It must be exciting to be a journalist." Jackie noticed a sour-faced Fallon seating herself at the far end of the table.

"You bet. And you? What's your line of work?"

She'd been ready for the question. "I'm between jobs right now. I've often thought about writing."

He laughed. "Most folks I meet say the same thing. What was your job back home?"

She ignored the question. "The more I think about it, the

more I like the idea. How did you get into the writing business, Mr. Lloyd?"

"Call me Byron." He took a sip of coffee. "I've done all kinds of things, just sort of fell into it."

"And what publication did you say you wrote for?"

"*Adventure Roads.* It's a nice little rag."

Jackie felt a presence at her elbow. She kept her body turned toward Lloyd, determined to wring more information out of the man, who she knew was not who he seemed to be.

Roman stood, shifting uneasily, a plate in his hands. Surely there was another place at the table somewhere. He found the benches filled with happy, munching people. The only available spot was next to Jackie, who seemed to be grilling Byron Lloyd. Roman was just about to turn around when Lloyd spotted him.

"Hey, young fella. Here's a seat for you." Lloyd shifted over and cleared a place between himself and Jackie.

"Don't worry about it. I'll eat in the kitchen."

"You'll do no such thing," said June Delucchi, replacing an empty platter of sausages with a steaming new batch. "The kitchen is insane. I've got breakfast going out and lunch already simmering, plus the baking to start for the snow-sculpture crowd. If you eat in there, you're liable to wind up in the stew pot."

Mr. Lloyd beamed. "Better not cross a lady with a knife collection."

Roman shot a glance at Jackie, who kept her gaze studiously fastened to her coffee cup. Sighing internally, he eased onto the bench, his arm tingling where it brushed against hers.

Lloyd clapped him on the back. "So, you two know each other, huh?"

Roman filled his mouth with eggs and nodded.

"Ever travel back to San Fran to visit her?"

He swallowed. "Only once a couple years ago." He'd sure imagined returning, though. How they'd see all the places she'd talked about. He didn't have much of a yen to travel, but for her, with her, anyplace would feel like home. The idea seemed like a child's fantasy to him now. To clear his head he took a deep swallow of coffee and burned his mouth.

Skip entered, frowning at a clipboard.

"Need some help, Skip?" Roman called over the clatter of the meal.

Skip looked up, momentarily disoriented. "No, no thanks. You eat your breakfast." He returned his attention to the clipboard and continued on toward the kitchen.

"He looks worried."

The soft voice surprised him. He looked at Jackie, who was following Skip's progress out of the room. "Yeah, I guess he does."

She kept her voice low. "Is the lodge business struggling?"

He shrugged. "It attracts a steady crowd, but the economy has hurt everyone." He wanted to say more, to keep her talking, but each word seemed a fresh reminder of what he'd had, and what he'd lost. It was too much. Picking up his plate, he made an excuse and stood up.

"What's the matter, man?" Lloyd boomed. "A strapping fellow like you can't live on two bites of breakfast."

"I've got a…" Roman's words were lost in a crash and shout from outside. He put his plate back on the table and ran out the front entrance, right behind Skip and June Delucchi, who had emerged from the kitchen. Jackie, Lloyd and a few other guests jogged out after them.

An overturned snowmobile lay on its side, engine sputtering. Nearby a groaning man clapped a hand to his leg. Dax, a handyman for the lodge, knelt next to the injured man. Skip ran to them.

"What's happened?"

Dax shook his head. "Reg hit a rock or something, maybe a buried tree limb. Snowmobile went over and I think he busted his ankle."

The man on the ground moaned. "Not busted, just sprained."

Roman hid a smile. Typical Alaska toughness. "Looks like there's some swelling. You need an X-ray, at least."

Talking over the grumbling from the stricken man, Skip and Dax made arrangements for Dax to drive to the nearest clinic. Reg was gingerly loaded onto a truck and sent off, in spite of his loud protests.

Roman looked at Skip and June. They'd moved away a piece and were having a serious conversation. He noticed June wiping away tears before she headed back to the lodge with the curious guests.

Jackie remained.

Roman put a hand on Skip's arm. "What can I do to help?"

Skip waved him off. "Nothing. You've already got more cargo to fly in for us."

"Not until later. I can help here." He gestured to the front loader. "I can fill some blocks while you go get the tape to mark it. We can find someone to stomp it down."

Skip shook his head. "I can't ask you to do that."

Roman headed toward the front loader. "You don't have to."

Skip gave him a grateful smile and left.

Before he started the engine, Roman looked up in surprise to find Jackie climbing the ladder perched against the wooden form farthest away from him.

"You don't have to do that, Jackie," he called. "I don't need help."

She looked up only for a moment. "Skip does," she yelled back.

That's right, Roman. She doesn't care about you anymore. That's the way it will always be. Get that through your thick head. His head already knew—it was his heart that needed convincing, he thought grimly, even after two long years.

Roman turned his attention to the front loader, fired the engine to life and began scooping up piles of snow and dumping them into the ten-foot wooden forms that would mold it into perfect blocks for sculpting. When one was relatively full, Jackie would climb up and stomp it all down before he added another load. When the snow was uncrated it would create perfect ten-foot-by-ten-foot squares. They kept at it. He could see the fatigue in her body, the tired droop to her head, yet she worked without complaint until June caught his eye from the front porch and gestured for them to come in for lunch.

Roman killed the motor and jumped down from the front loader. His hands were stiff. They'd filled only eleven of the boxes completely—still another five to go. He made his way over to Jackie, who had not seen June's summons. She was busily stomping down snow with a vengeance.

"Jackie? Lunch-break command from Mrs. D."

She nodded and began to climb down the ladder. As she did so, the ladder pitched loose from the side of the box and wobbled, causing her to lose her footing. Jackie slipped, maintaining her grip on the ladder with only one hand, until she fell.

There wasn't time to think about it. Roman caught her as they tumbled to the ground. She landed next to him, eyes wide, lips parted in shock. The feel of her small frame against his side, the softness of her hair tickling his chin drowned him in memory for a moment. He could have imagined it, but for the briefest second he felt her lean her head against his shoulder.

With a sudden movement she scrambled to her feet. Roman did the same. Jackie turned to face him, her cheeks flushed a deep crimson. "Thanks…I, I must be tired to fall off a ladder."

He shrugged, hoping she could not read his feelings on his face. "You've been working hard. No harm done."

Jackie giggled. "Sorry, but you've got a clump of snow stuck right to the top of your head."

He held still while she reached out and brushed the snow off his hair.

He flushed and let her finish.

"Thanks again, for the soft landing." She turned and started toward the lodge, pulling her gloves off and unzipping her pocket to put them inside. As she did so something small and metallic spiraled down. Jackie started frantically, twirling around, peering at the snow-covered ground to find the item. Her face was stark, body tense.

Roman joined her in the search. "What fell?"

"Nothing. Nothing important."

The lie was obvious in her increasing panic. He bent over to squint at the harshly glittering snow until he saw the item and picked it up. He didn't get time to look closely, as she snatched it from his fingers.

"Thanks. That's it. Um, thank you. Thanks again." Without a word of explanation, she jogged toward the building, leaving him to wonder.

Whatever was on that thumb drive, she acted like it was a matter of life and death.

FIVE

She couldn't get over the fear that had enveloped her when she'd dropped the thumb drive. And Roman—what had he thought when he retrieved it for her? She could still feel his big hands on her waist, trying to catch her as she fell. Those hands had comforted her through her entire youth, it seemed. For a split second she wished with every pore of her body that things had been different.

She made her way to her room with a tray of food provided by June and shot an uneasy glance at the sky, a brilliant blue that seemed to shimmer with intensity. She'd heard one of the kitchen staff mention that a blizzard was in the forecast, but she hoped it wasn't true. Skip was counting on a successful snow-sculpture weekend, and she prayed he would get it.

Cresting the small ridge to her cabin, she was startled to see two people making their way in the deep snow off the path. The snowshoes strapped to their feet gave them a comical gait. It was Byron Lloyd and a smaller figure who it took her a moment to identify. Fallon. They both waved.

Jackie watched Fallon for a moment. The girl's face was thrown back in laughter. She was a young woman, no longer a child, but there was still plenty of the girl showing through. Jackie's heart squeezed, thinking about how much Danny's death must have hurt Fallon. Jackie had been so wrapped in her own grief and anger, she hadn't given much thought to Fallon's.

Shaking her head to clear it, she unlocked the door to her cabin. Her stomach clenched as she stuck the key in and found the door already unlocked. As it swung open, all of her plans were forgotten. She screamed.

Skip made it to her cabin first, still holding a half-eaten sandwich in his hand, but Roman was close behind. Jackie stood immobile in the center of the room, surveying the damage around her. The contents of her bag were scattered over the bed, shirts, socks and pants draping the coverlet. The bathroom medicine cabinet was open and her few toiletries in disarray.

Skip swallowed the bite he'd been chewing. "What in the world?"

Roman moved closer and spoke softly. "Someone was looking for something. Anything taken that you can tell?"

Her eyes darted to the computer, the only real thing of value besides the satellite phone she'd had in her backpack. Both were still there, but the computer was on. She breathed a quick prayer of thanks that she'd deleted the message Asia had sent. But what if Asia had forwarded more while she was helping pile snow? What had the intruder seen? Her skin prickled, and she itched to scan her inbox but with Roman and Skip there, she didn't dare.

"No, nothing taken." She felt a shudder sweep through her, and she wrapped her arms around herself to hold it in.

Skip shook his head. "Never in the years I've owned this place has something like this happened. Whoever it was must have picked the lock or gotten the spare from the lodge office." He sighed. "We'll have to go to the police when we're in town. See what they make of it."

Jackie jumped. Was she ready to explain to the cops? How

could she tell them about the break-in without revealing the whole sordid mess? "No, I don't think that's necessary."

Skip stared at her. "Why not?"

She forced a laugh. "It's probably just a prank. There was no harm done, nothing stolen, no one hurt." But it wasn't a prank. The person who'd been snooping on her laptop hadn't found what they were after, so they'd come back and searched more thoroughly.

Roman raised an eyebrow, but didn't speak. He cocked his head and his long bangs shadowed his face. Jackie wished she could read his thoughts.

Skip looked unconvinced. "Well, if you're sure, I certainly have other things to focus on today. I'd put you in another cabin, but we're full up. In any case, I've got one of those latch locks we can add. I can try to get Dax to install it."

"I'll do it."

Roman's voice was so low she almost didn't hear it.

Skip shot a glance at him and then at Jackie. "I'd sure appreciate it, Roman. I'd never ask, but I'm just plain swamped."

"I'll do it after my last flight this afternoon."

Skip nodded and headed for the door. "I'm awful sorry about this, Jackie. I hope it doesn't ruin your vacation. I can't imagine who would do such a thing and why." He plodded out into the snow.

At that moment her phone rang. She moved to a corner to answer, hands shaking.

"Ms. Swann?" The voice was muffled.

"Who is calling?"

"Officer Smith, S.F.P.D. We've been looking for you. We have some questions about the situation at your employer's."

Something in the stilted tone made her uneasy. "Okay, but first tell me the name of your supervising officer and your badge number."

There was a long moment of silence. "You are the one being questioned here."

"Not until you give me the information."

The tone of the voice changed. "Look, honey. We know where you live and the make and model of your car. We even know where your father lives. All we want is that thumb drive. You hand that over and you get your life back."

Her stomach spasmed. "Don't threaten me," she snapped.

"We'll get to you. It's a matter of time. You'd better keep your mouth shut."

She hung up, head spinning. Reynolds's men knew she was here. Had they paid someone at the lodge to search her room? Or sent one of their own men? She thought of Byron Lloyd.

Her knees began to tremble with a sudden violence. Before she sank to the floor, Roman caught her and helped her to a chair. She sat there clinging to his hand, terror threatening to sweep her away.

He knelt next to her, eyes searching, and gently stroked her hand.

"What is it?" he whispered. "What is wrong, Jackie?"

She clutched his fingers, trying to will his strength into her body. It was too much. She'd gotten herself into a place she could not get out of. They would find her. She shivered. They already had. "I don't know what to do."

He frowned. "About what?" He leaned closer. "Tell me, Jackie. Let me help you."

His face shone with concern. If she could just lean on him, trust him as she had for so many years. Her father's words came back to her. *Roman killed your brother. Don't ever forget that.* Though she wanted more than anything to lay her burden on his wide shoulders, she could not. Not with Roman. Allowing him into her life again would reopen wounds that were still ragged with agony. With a painful effort, she pulled her hand out of his grasp. "Nothing. A delayed reaction to all this. I'm okay."

"You don't look okay."

She forced herself to breath normally, to still the shaking of her hands. "Really, I'm fine."

"No, you're not. If you don't want to share your problem with me, I guess I can understand that." His eyes clouded. "I know that all ended a long time ago, but maybe you'd better confide in someone who can help you." He gestured around the room. "This looks like more than you can handle on your own."

Her whirl of emotion exploded into a fiery rage. "Don't tell me what I can or can't do. I've handled it all, including laying my brother to rest. And where were you, Roman? You were nowhere. Did you call? Write? Did you even think about how I was handling things without my brother and my father, sick with grief?" She found herself sobbing.

Roman looked as if he'd been punched. "I'm sorry. I wanted to talk to you, but I couldn't think of anything to say that wouldn't hurt you more. I wrote, but I never mailed the letters."

"You just didn't want to face up to what you did."

He shook his head. "I've had to face up to that every day, every minute of my life." He started toward the door and continued, his voice almost a whisper. "Just so you know, I visit the spot where you scattered Danny's ashes all the time. And I was there that day, at the funeral, watching from the bluff."

She almost didn't hear his last words. "I think I died that day, too."

"I…I didn't know. You should have come to me at the funeral."

His eyes glittered. "Come to you? Would you have wanted the person who killed your brother there? Would your father?"

She couldn't answer.

He sighed. "That's what I thought. I've got to go now."

After he'd left she tried to still the trembling that swept

through her. He'd been there, on that terrible day, enduring the grief and shouldering his own deep sense of guilt. She had never known that he'd shared the blackest moment of her life.

The idea was too much, too dark.

Desperately she tried to direct her mind to something else.

With shaking hands, she nudged the computer to life, praying a new message from Asia hadn't arrived when the intruder was in the cabin. It seemed an eternity before the in-box swam into view. No new messages.

The relief took her breath away. She pulled up a search engine and input *Adventure Roads Magazine*.

"Let's see if you're telling the truth, Mr. Lloyd." The Web site was slick and colorful. Part of her felt disappointed. She'd been half expecting to find there was no such magazine, but here it was in bold, splashy color. An online archive made it easy to search all prior issues.

This time when the search was finished, Jackie felt not disappointment, but sick dread. There wasn't one single article by anyone named Byron Lloyd.

Roman had a hard time keeping his mind on his work as he checked over the plane.

Jackie was terrified of someone, perhaps the same someone who had broken into her room. He fought a strong desire to return to check on her, call her, drop everything and find her that very moment.

Jackie felt like he'd abandoned her, killed her brother and left her to handle the grief alone. He slammed the toolbox shut. The past couldn't be changed, but what about the present situation? Who was after her? And why? Even the thrum of the plane's engines when he fired them to life a half hour later did not calm his thoughts. He noted the increasing cloud cover. Possible blizzard approaching.

It would be devastating for Skip and the snow-sculpture competition. With each competitor forking over several hundred dollars to participate, Skip would get to keep a nice chunk of the entry fee to cover costs. He'd also make a hefty bit of change selling food—if the weather didn't interfere. Roman hoped the blizzard held off. Skip seemed stressed and distracted lately. He didn't need anything else on his plate. Skip was like a father to him. He couldn't bear to see him so pained. Roman's own father was only a distant memory, a man who'd left when he was just a kid.

He was surprised to see Jackie with Skip as they approached the cleared landing strip.

He opened the passenger-side door for her. "You going along?"

She nodded, her face screened by a curtain of coppery hair and showing no signs of her earlier outburst. "I've got to do some business at the bank."

He wondered, but didn't question as they flew toward the airport. "Skip and I have to get the supplies loaded, then I can drive us into town. Okay by you, Skip?"

The man looked up from a piece of paper he'd been perusing. "What?"

Roman repeated the plan.

"Sure, sure. That's fine." He returned his attention to the paper.

Jackie turned. "Everything okay, Skip? You seem worried about something."

Skip started. "Who me? Nah. Just all the fuss about Winter-fest. I'm fine."

Jackie faced front again but Roman saw her looking at Skip in the side mirror. She too felt there was something not quite right. Roman tried to keep his mind fixed firmly on the approaching airport, though the scent of Jackie's newly washed hair triggered a cascade of memories. He remembered how it had looked at the funeral; smooth, twisted into a coil of fire that glimmered in the sunlight.

Not now, Roman. Not ever.

They landed and jogged through the frigid air into the loading area. Crates of fresh vegetables, flour and sugar and frozen meats were ready and waiting. Skip arranged for signatures, and Roman waved to Al as the heavyset man climbed onto a forklift. After he finished the paperwork, Skip climbed up a ladder to a landing ten feet above them, and began sorting the crates into efficient stacks.

Roman turned to Jackie to tell her there was coffee in the terminal but found her busily scanning a message board that flashed the incoming and outgoing flights. Her face was drawn in a look of such concentration, he started over to see exactly what had caught her interest so completely. He'd made it only a few steps when a cry made him turn.

The forklift lurched unexpectedly backward and toppled, sending the machine over. The violent jerk made Skip lose his balance. He yelled, holding desperately onto the edge of the landing, dangling in the air.

Al struggled to free himself from the overturned equipment. Roman ran to cut the engine on the forklift while he yelled to Skip, "Hang on."

Skip would not be able to maintain his grip for long. A ten-foot fall onto a stack of wooden crates might just break the man's back.

"I'll go to the ladder," Jackie yelled, running across the lot to a ladder fixed to the far side of the loading dock.

"No time." Roman climbed on the tipped forklift and eased his way onto the nearest stack of boxes. They shifted ominously under his feet. Pulse pounding, he leaped onto a stack of crates a second before the one he was standing on gave way with a lurch. Boxes toppled down underneath him but Roman's eyes were fixed on the man who desperately gripped the landing ledge a few feet above him.

Continuing up as quickly as he could, Roman crawled across the stacked boxes and with the biggest leap he could manage, hurled himself onto the platform. He made it, barely. Muscles straining, he hoisted a leg over the ledge, then the other and scrambled over to the spot where Skip struggled to hang on.

Grasping Skip by both wrists, Roman kept his own body as close to the landing as possible to keep from being pulled over the edge. With every bit of strength left, he hauled Skip back onto the platform. They both lay there for a moment, sweating and panting. Jackie made it up the ladder and ran over to them.

Jackie's face was white as she knelt next to Roman and Skip, trying to assess both men at once. "Are you hurt?"

Roman closed his eyes against the dizziness that made his head swim, not from the exertion, but from the nearness of her, the small hand on his arm, the brush of her hair on his face. "Not hurt," he managed.

Skip also groaned a reassurance and managed to sit up. When he turned to look at Roman, a strange wash of emotion flowed over his face. "You, you saved me."

Roman cleared his throat. "You would have been fine."

Skip continued to stare, his eyes fixed in terrible concentration. "No, I wouldn't. You shouldn't have done it, Roman, not for me."

Roman thought for a horrifying moment the man was going to cry until Jackie knelt by him. She had noticed Skip's strange reaction too. "Are you sure you're okay?"

Skip shook his head and nodded, wiping a hand across his forehead. He hauled himself up and headed for the ladder. Jackie stared after him, a puzzled look on her face, then she turned to Roman and stroked his shoulder. "Are you sure you aren't hurt?"

He wanted to hold her hand there forever. "Not hurt."

"That was crazy. What were you thinking?"

The words came out before he had a chance to strip out the emotion. "I was thinking I could save him."

She must have heard it in his tone, the thought that rose to the surface like a needle-toothed barracuda. *Like I tried to save your brother.*

The pain flashed in the amber depths of her eyes. She jerked her hand away and stood. The moment was gone, Jackie was gone, and he felt only a heavy fatigue, weightier than the snow that had buried them on that terrible night.

SIX

Whe hen the loading was done, they made their way to town in a Wayne's Aviation van. Jackie mulled over the accident at the airport. Roman's behavior had been reckless. She felt a surge of anger. How had he felt when his recklessness had caused him to drive off the road with her brother in the car? He'd said he couldn't remember the details. There was some mysterious vehicle that appeared and caused them to veer over the embankment. Rescuers and investigators had found no sign of any such thing. It was an excuse, a way to escape blame that should rest entirely on his shoulders.

Please, Lord. Take my anger away. She'd asked God countless times already to free her from the rage that burned brightly inside her. There was something that prevented her from letting it go, a heavy weight that kept her anger fixed firmly in place.

She thought of Skip's face as he lay on the platform, a mixture of relief and gratitude and another emotion that she couldn't define. Something was definitely not right with Skip Delucchi. She turned it over and over in her mind before her thoughts led her back to Roman.

It might have been a rash act, but she had to admit it was also a selfless one. Much easier to wait until help arrived, to climb the safer route as they had, knowing Skip would have fallen before aid arrived.

She looked surreptitiously at Roman, who kept his eyes fixed on the snowy road. He had always been impulsive, but there was a calmer quality to him now, and a sober maturity in his face. For a moment, she had the wildest urge, in spite of her anger, to reach out and touch the strong fingers that gripped the steering wheel.

Snap out of it, Jackie. You're losing your sanity. She fingered the thumb drive in her pocket as they rumbled into town.

"Going to the Sea Mart to get something," Skip said, his face still a shade too pale, Jackie thought.

Roman nodded. "I'm going that way too." He shot a look at Jackie.

She waved them off. "I've got banking to do. I'll meet you back at the van."

They disembarked into an intense cold that made her eyes tear. As Skip hopped out, he dropped his bundled papers. An envelope hit the ground, scattering its contents.

Jackie barely restrained a gasp to see a dozen hundred-dollar bills fluttering in the slight breeze. She and Roman helped Skip retrieve the money before it could blow away.

Skip's face reddened. "Gotta make a payment. Cash seems like the easiest thing." Without another word he shoved the bundle into his pocket and headed toward the grocery store.

Jackie saw the worried frown on Roman's face, which she knew matched the one on her own.

She shook her head. "That's a lot of cash."

"Uh-huh. Sure is." Jackie watched Roman's tall form as he walked away across the street. He wore only a light windbreaker, his body perfectly acclimated to the freezing temperatures. Shivering, she zipped her coat, wishing she could face the cold as bravely.

The clerk at the bank greeted her with impersonal efficiency. She was grateful not to run into anyone she'd known two years prior. The man issued her a small safe-deposit box and with great relief she deposited the thumb drive. It might be the only proof they could find that Reynolds was bilking his clients. Had he sent the threatening message? In spite of the warm air in the bank, she shivered, casting a glance around to see if anyone was watching as she strolled back through the lobby and out the front door.

Blinking in the sunshine, Jackie saw Roman loading a bag into the back of the van. Skip had not returned. What business would he have that would require him to carry so much cash around? Remote Alaska was very much a cash-and-carry place, but he'd behaved so oddly after the accident and in the van she didn't think it was an ordinary debt.

She started to make her way back to the van when someone grabbed her arm. Crying out, she whirled to find herself staring into the exuberant face of Mick Andrade.

"Mick!" She hugged him tightly, noting the bruise on his cheekbone from the beating. "I'm so glad to see you. How did you find me? Where's Asia?"

Mick gave her a hearty squeeze and shook his head, speaking in a low tone. "I got in last night. Asia isn't here—she's coming on a later flight. She called your father in Maryland. Apparently the owner's wife called to let him know you'd arrived safely."

Jackie groaned. It probably hadn't occurred to June that Jackie wouldn't want her father to know her whereabouts.

He looked over her shoulder and an expression of concern flitted across his face. "Who's the big guy?"

Jackie saw Roman striding toward them. "He's…a friend. Tell me about Asia."

"Not here," he whispered. "She's okay, but I need to talk to you in private."

Roman joined them and introduced himself. "Who's this?"

Was she imagining it, or was there a subtle look of challenge on Roman's face? "This is Mick Andrade. We work together in San Francisco."

"Nice to meet you." Roman shook his hand. "What brings you to Alaska?"

Mick gave him an easy smile. "Heard all about this Winterfest celebration and I thought I'd check it out."

Roman nodded. "It's a great vacation if you're into the outdoors."

Mick straightened. "That's me—grew up in Wyoming. These winters have got nothing on Wyoming winters."

Roman nodded. "Give it a few days and see if you still think so."

Jackie was relieved when Skip arrived. She repeated the introductions.

Skip listened attentively. "Pleasure to meet any friend of Jackie's. So, where are you staying, Mick? I'd put you up in one of our units, but the lodge is booked."

He laughed. "Let me know if something opens up, but I'm not sure I could afford the rates, anyway. Some old-timer rented me his hunting cabin up behind your place, I think. Really in the boonies. He loaned me his snowmobile too."

Roman raised an eyebrow. "Can you drive one? Not as easy as it looks."

Mick smiled. "I can handle anything with an engine."

Skip cleared his throat. "You lookin' for work at all, Mick? I got a bunch more to be done tonight. It's hard work, I'll warn you. Tough stuff."

"That would be great. I'd be happy to do whatever you need."

Skip sighed in relief. "Music to my ears. I can have one of the guys take you back to your cabin later."

"Sounds good to me. Let's go."

They piled into the van, Skip in front with Roman, Jackie and Mick in the backseat and Mick's snowmobile attached to the rear bumper. Jackie was dying to question him, but there was no way to keep from being overheard. Roman already looked as if a thundercloud hovered over his head. She didn't want him privy to any more details about her situation. She could see by the look on Mick's face he had plenty to tell her.

Roman flew them all back to the lodge and busied himself unloading supplies as the sun sank behind the horizon. He kept a close eye on Mick, as Skip put him speedily to work filling the boxes with the front loader. Jackie volunteered to stomp snow. Was it an excuse to stay close to Mick? Who was the guy, anyway? Roman didn't buy the whole winter vacation thing for a minute. The dude was too citified to be an outdoorsman. Still, Roman had to admit, he knew how to work a front loader.

With no other flights to attend to, Roman helped out moving heavy crates from the back room to the kitchen for June Delucchi. He volunteered to string lights across the front of the lodge in order to keep Jackie and Mick in his line of sight. If Mick was Jackie's boyfriend, he'd know it soon enough. And if he was? Roman's hands stopped in midair, strings of lights dangling from his fingers. If Mick and Jackie were together, there wouldn't be a single thing he could do about it. He had no right to interfere. No right, yet the feelings swelled anyway, the bond between them, the past they'd shared was too hard to forget, for him anyway.

Couldn't she at least have picked a guy with some substance to him? Mick was a dark-haired beanpole and Roman knew he wouldn't last a day in the Alaskan wilderness, in spite of his confidence. The thought eased his mind as he finished stringing the lights.

Mick eventually headed off with Dax to retrieve his snow-mobile and return to the hunting lodge. Roman was pleased the guy hadn't agreed to stay for dinner. Jackie went inside at June's insistence to warm up.

Roman uncrated the snow molds into precise, sparkling cubes, ready for sculpting. Skip practically beamed.

"Didn't think we were going to make it. Just in time, too."

The sky was completely dark, illuminated only by a wedge of moon showing between the clouds and Roman's newly affixed lights. Several dozen people scurried along the ridge at the northern edge of the property where the land sloped gently upward to a bank of trees. Some were artists but most were eager bystanders. They'd erected tents, and a few enterprising visitors even constructed their own igloos, intent on staying the night.

Roman heard the strum of a guitar and saw candle-powered lanterns flicker to life. He watched in admiration as two people finished their snow shelter. With a pang he remembered showing Jackie how to build an igloo. Their first effort had been a bit lopsided, but the look of pride on her face when they'd finished overshadowed any imperfections. She'd looked as beautiful as an Alaska sunrise. She'd thrown her arms around him, and he'd known what pure joy felt like.

He turned away from the festive scene and made his way into the lodge.

The first batch of guests was already enjoying June's pot roast and garlic potatoes. Jackie was not in the dining area. In the kitchen, June was tending to multiple pots. He grabbed a stack of dirty pots and set to work, hoping Jackie would make an appearance for the second dinner-shift.

June took a moment to wrap him in a hug and plant a kiss on his cheek. "What did we do to deserve you, honey?"

Deserve him? He wondered if Jackie said the same thing,

only with an entirely different inflection. Her father certainly hadn't been shy after the accident.

You killed my son. You're no better than a murderer.

When the mountain of dishware was washed and drying on a rack, there was still no sign of Jackie. Had she gone back to her cabin? With a start he remembered he hadn't changed the lock on her cabin door. He excused himself and retrieved the new hardware from the utility closet.

The sky was alight with a cathedral of stars that peeked between the clouds. The revelers were louder now, music played and people arrived by snowmobile, until there was quite a crowd milling about, dancing and laughing. Skip left the lodge carrying a tray laden with tin coffee cups for the visitors.

Roman crunched along the path with his toolbox. No light shone from Jackie's cabin. When he drew close, Lloyd's door opened and the man greeted him. Had he been watching through the window?

"Hey, young fella. There's a party getting started over there. Are you going to join in?"

"No, not tonight. I'm sure they'd welcome you, though. Why don't you go and get some material for your article?"

"Good idea. But I need a date." He laughed at his joke. "Think the lovely Miss Swann would accompany an old man like myself?"

Roman hesitated. "I'm not sure. You'd have to ask her."

Lloyd made his way through the snow to knock on Jackie's door.

No answer.

"Maybe she's already headed over there," Lloyd said, a frown on his face. "Or did she go off to visit that work friend of hers?"

"No." He realized he'd spoken sharply so he gentled his tone. "No, I'm sure she's around here somewhere."

"She's a hard one to keep track of."

Why do you want to keep track of her? He decided the question was too direct. The man was jovial—lonely probably. It was his line of work to be nosy. Lloyd disappeared in his cabin and returned bundled in a heavy jacket. "I'll go stag, then."

Roman watched him leave before he knocked again on Jackie's door. Using the key Skip had given him he unlocked it and called into the gap, "Jackie? It's Roman. I'm going to change your lock, okay?"

Receiving no answer he eased into the cabin. Her computer was off and the room was cold. He edged the thermostat up and set to work on the lock.

When the project was finished and he'd tarried as long as he dared, he returned the tools to the lodge, hung the new key on the peg in the office and wandered outside, toward Jackie's favorite spot.

The bluff was a gentle rise of rock that sheltered the lodge from the worst of the winter winds. It rose to a towering peak that was completely buried under a crystal crust of snow. At the bottom of the bluff were several acres thickly populated with pine trees, often home to deer in the summer, the occasional family of brown bears and a perpetual scattering of moose. Jackie had always loved the spot, climbing to the top of the bluff to see the panorama of the Alaskan wild all around her.

The snow was hard packed, but he still wished he'd brought his snowshoes as he sank with each step. He finally caught a glimpse of her. She stood, head bent in thought, something in her hand that looked like a phone. Her jacket gleamed in the moonlight.

He was transported back into their past when she had been a part of this world. Her laughter and wide smile came to him as if no time had passed. The sky seemed to echo his feelings as a cloud passed over the moon and turned the snow from silver to deepest gray. He thought he saw movement in the thick cluster of trees above her. It was probably a bird or a rabbit, but something about he flicker struck him as odd. He hastened up the slope toward Jackie.

SEVEN

She'd given Mick her satellite phone number. He'd promised to call later and fill her in on the problems back home and, most importantly, Asia's situation. Her mind whirled with too much conjecture. Why hadn't Asia flown out with Mick? Was she looking into something further? Had it been too dangerous for them to be seen together?

As revelers and snow sculptors began to arrive in droves, Jackie had sought the solitude of her favorite spot. The bluff was so perfect, so pristine that it had always been a place that quieted her nerves. At the moment, her nerves were in serious need of quieting. The hissed message on her answering machine kept playing in her mind.

Your father will pay.

She'd thought Alaska would be the perfect place to disappear, but Asia had found her and so had Mick…and whoever the angry voice on her machine belonged to, and potentially Byron Lloyd. Maybe she should have stayed in San Francisco, gone to the police. The details pinwheeled and overwhelmed her.

She didn't even realize where she was headed as her feet took her farther away from the cabin. She stayed to the rocky margins of a twisted path, intending to turn around if the snow became too soft and thick to traverse.

A strange noise in the distance made her stop. Heart in her throat, she froze. Was it a bear? A moose? The crunch of snow continued in a steady rhythm that sounded decidedly unbear-like. Whatever or whoever approached was big.

In her panic she considered running, but making any kind of speed in snow would be impossible. Calling for help would be her best option. If she could get someone to answer at the lodge…at least tell them where she was. Berating herself for wandering off alone, she tried to dial with shaking fingers.

The figure emerged into view. Relief flooded through her when she recognized Roman's broad shoulders and sweep of dark hair. She saw him open his mouth to call to her, his hand half raised in greeting, and then a shot exploded in her ears.

She thought she must be dreaming. The sound made her ears ring. She felt a pressure on her shoulder and then Roman burst to life, hurtling into her and knocking her to the ground. Snow closed around her in an icy shroud and Roman's heavy body rendered her immobile.

"Stay down," he whispered, his voice low and urgent. "Someone's shooting."

Shooting? The word didn't make sense to her shocked mind. Who would be shooting?

After a moment, Roman rolled off her, picked her up and sprinted to the shelter of the rocky bluff. He put her carefully against a shelf of snow and knelt, peering into her face.

"Are you hurt, Jackie?"

The tender worry on his face took her breath away and she could not answer. She felt his hands on her arms, gently checking for injury. He stopped when he got to her right shoulder. The look on his face became grave. When he pulled his hand away from her jacket, she could see his fingers stained with blood. Her blood.

"Somebody shot me?" Her voice was no louder than a whisper.

He gripped her arms. "It's going to be all right. You're going to be okay. Stay awake for me."

His voice wrapped her in a silky caress. For a moment she let herself slide into the comfort of his touch. Her body began to shiver, to convulse into shudders that vibrated her whole body. From some distant place came the roar of snowmobiles, then the sound of feet moving rapidly across the snow. Anxious voices drifted through the cold air. She did not hear any more as she sank into unconsciousness.

Some distant part of Roman's mind registered the crowd of visitors running toward them, ringing the area with shocked faces. Skip pushed through and gaped.

"What happened? I thought I heard a shot."

"You did. Jackie's been hit," Roman snapped. "We've got to get her to the plane, fly her to Mercy." His nerves felt like they were on fire. All he could think of was getting her to safety.

Lloyd arrived, pink-cheeked and panting. "A shot? Could it have been someone after bears?"

Fallon picked her way to Roman and handed him a pair of snowshoes.

Someone offered Roman a scarf and he wrapped Jackie's shoulder as tightly as he could. He strapped on the snowshoes and Skip and Lloyd helped him lift Jackie onto a collapsible stretcher someone had fetched from the lodge. If the bullet had been a few inches to the left… He shut down the thought.

In a moment, he'd taken one end of the stretcher, and someone he didn't know took the other. He dared only one glance back at Jackie. Her face was pale as milk, eyes closed. They half marched, half jogged through the snow to the plane. Nighttime wasn't the best for flying, but at least the blizzard was holding off.

He started the engines, and Skip climbed in the back next to

Jackie. Fallon hopped in the front and strapped in. Roman barely felt the sweat on his brow from carrying Jackie to the plane at full speed. He was only aware of an enormous urgency pushing him along, like a skier running in front of an avalanche.

Save her.

He wasn't sure if the plea was meant for himself or for God, but the thought ran again and again through his mind.

Save her, please.

He fought against the frustration of not being able to hold her hand, to comfort her. She wouldn't want you to, he reminded himself.

Fallon cast an uneasy glance toward the backseat. "There's not too much blood."

He knew from the amount of blood, and the location of the shot, that it was not a life-threatening wound but he also knew that shock could kill a person as effectively as any bullet.

"Keep her warm," he called to Skip.

"She's bundled up to the chin."

He radioed their position, and the hospital confirmed they'd have an ambulance waiting at the landing strip.

True to their word, he saw the red lights as the wheels touched down on the newly cleared runway. In a blur of activity, paramedics loaded Jackie into the ambulance and whisked her away, leaving Roman, Skip and Fallon to follow in a hospital-provided van.

It was a surreal dream—a nightmare, in fact. The walls of the hospital loomed over them, and the night of the accident that had killed Danny was all brought back in horrible detail.

Was he about to experience the nightmare anew? Was it Jackie, this time, who would be cut away from his life? His gut twisted. Anything but that. Anything.

Save her, please. This time, though he knew he did not deserve any favors, the plea was meant for God.

Skip and Roman sat in hard, green chairs in a waiting room that smelled of burnt coffee. Fifteen minutes into their stay, and Roman was up and pacing. He walked as far as the cold tile hallway would allow before he made his way back in the other direction. He couldn't escape the black cloud of fear. On his fourth time around, Fallon fell into place next to him.

"Feel bad?"

He nodded.

She hugged herself. "I hate this place. Reminds me of the accident."

He clamped his mouth together, not trusting himself to answer.

She went on. "That night, Mom brought me down as soon as we got the call. I couldn't believe it. Cops said you were driving the truck and swerved off the road."

"So I've heard." His voice was bitter.

"You told everyone that there was another car or truck or something stopped in the road that caused the accident."

Closing his eyes, he could see it, a gleam of metal appearing suddenly around a sharp corner. He heard himself slamming on the brakes and the sudden spill of snow that swept them along in a relentless tide. The twist of metal, the breaking of glass and then silence. Was it real? Or was it his mind fashioning a way to ease his guilt? They'd told him the concussion he'd sustained had interfered with his memory. Someday his brain might be able to reconstruct the accident, or he might live his whole life and never unscramble the images of that night.

Fallon gripped his arm suddenly, fingers rigid. "I believe you, Roman, about what happened."

He tried to decipher the intense expression on her face. "Sometimes I'm not sure whether I believe it or not. It's all so foggy."

Her hand dropped and her eyes filled with tears. "It's not your fault he's dead."

"I appreciate that, Fallon, but…"

Her words came out in a whisper. "It's mine."

For a moment all he could do was gape at her. "What do you mean? You weren't anywhere near that accident." In spite of the curiosity her words had awakened in him, he wanted to ease the discomfort on her face. She was still a child, as much as she pretended not to be.

They grew silent as Skip approached. He eyed Fallon carefully as he spoke. "The doc has news for us."

They hustled to the waiting area and met the green-clad physician. She smiled reassuringly. "Ms. Swann is going to be fine. The wound was superficial, only a few stitches. We're going to give her fluids and keep her overnight for observation, but I expect tomorrow she'll be good to go."

Roman's relief almost choked him. "Can I see her?"

"Sure. But only one of you at a time and only for a few minutes. She's groggy from the painkillers."

Roman looked at Skip.

"Go on. You go check on her. I've got to call June and fill her in."

Roman made his way into the dim hospital room. Jackie looked very small under the thick blanket. She stirred when he touched her arm.

"Hey, there. You scared us good this time."

She opened her eyes and smiled faintly. "I'm fine."

He laughed. "That's what I figured you'd say. I'm glad to hear the doctor confirm your diagnosis anyway. You had us all worried for a while there."

She closed her eyes and Roman thought she might fall asleep. There was one thing he had to know.

"Jackie?"

"Hmm?"

"Do you remember what happened?"

Her eyes fluttered open and she nodded. "There was a shot."

"Yeah. Rifle shot. Knicked you on the shoulder. Lloyd thought it might be a bear hunter, but we know better than that."

Her expression grew wary. "Probably an accident."

"Maybe," he said. *Unlikely,* his gut added. "You were all alone out there, at the bluff. What for?"

She shrugged. "Needed solitude."

"When I saw you, you had a satellite phone in your hand."

He saw the stubborn set to her face, the shadow of fear behind her eyes that he knew would keep her from telling him the truth. But he had to know. He had to make sure she was safe.

"Jackie, this is getting serious. Whatever you're hiding almost got you killed. Now, who were you expecting a call from?"

The voice surprised them both.

"From me," Mick said, as he stepped into the room.

EIGHT

Jackie's head snapped around to the door. Mick's cheeks were reddened and his jacket was still speckled with bits of snow. He walked past Roman to the bed, eyes wide. "Are you all right? Mrs. Delucchi told me about the accident. I snowmobiled over, but it took me forever."

"I'm okay."

He sank into a hard chair next to the bed. "I feel terrible." He shot a look at Roman. "She was waiting for my call. We made arrangements to catch up. Thinking of you out there getting shot while you waited for me gives me the creeps." He shook his head. "What happened? Someone playing around with a rifle?"

Roman snorted. "People here don't play around with guns. They're tools and they're treated that way. It wasn't an accident. The police will investigate. Skip's already called them."

Jackie's stomach flipped at the thought of talking to the police. She knew he was probably right, but for the moment all she wanted to do was find out about Asia.

Roman's phone rang and he stepped into the hallway to answer it.

Mick leaned toward the bed. "I thought he'd never get out of here. He your boyfriend?"

She swallowed. "No, but he used to be, a long time ago. It's over now."

Mick raised an eyebrow. "I don't think it's over on his end."

She shifted a shiver. "Never mind that. Where's Asia?"

He held up a hand. "Still in San Francisco."

Jackie gaped. "I don't understand. Why didn't she come with you?"

He stood and walked to a small window. "Because she's as stubborn as you are. She was sure that she was close to finding concrete proof in that mountain of notes. She wanted to put it all together so we could go to the authorities."

"Is it safe for her to stay alone?"

"Safe?" He passed a hand over his eyes and she saw a heavy fatigue on his face. "I wouldn't say that. Right after you left someone tried to drive us off the road."

Jackie gasped.

"Yeah. We only barely made it out of that scrape. The car was a sedan, male driver, but I know it was an unmarked police car. Cops are dirty, all right."

Jackie felt like jumping out of the bed and grabbing him by the jacket. "Where is Asia? We've got to get her out of there."

"She begged me to come take care of you, to find a place for us all to hole up. Then she just took off, left a note that she went to a friend's. She's driving me crazy." Mick sighed. "I wish I knew where she was."

Jackie almost smiled. Asia was stubborn without question. "She's good at landing on her feet."

Mick patted her hand. "The sooner we get this taken care of, the better. What have you been able to put together?"

"Nothing, so far. I know the answer is on that drive. Someone else knows it too. There was a break-in at my cabin."

He started. "At the lodge? Who would do that?"

"I'm not sure, but I think it might be one of the guests there who is passing himself off as a reporter."

His eyes rolled in thought. "Dr. Reynolds must have figured out where you went and paid someone off. A local cop, maybe. The people he's selling the information to must have a long reach, and they don't want their operation compromised. Where's the evidence? We have to make sure it's safe."

She opened her mouth to reply when a nurse stepped in.

"Visiting hours are over in ten minutes."

Mick started to protest, but Jackie cut him off. "It's okay. I'll be fine here for the night."

"What are you going to tell the police?" he whispered.

"Maybe I should tell them everything."

His dark eyes gleamed with worry. "Not with Asia unprotected. The Alaska cops will immediately contact SFPD and they'll find her. We've got to wait until she's here and safe. I told her if she didn't fly out pronto I was going to come back for her."

Roman returned then, hovering uncertainly in the doorway until Mick left. He bobbed a chin in the direction Mick had taken. "He looks worried."

She sighed. "He's concerned about me and his girlfriend, Asia."

Roman raised an eyebrow. "His girlfriend?"

"Oh." His gaze wandered all over the room. "I just wanted to tell you I'll come back tomorrow to pick you up, if that's what you want." He turned to go.

"Wait." Jackie felt an inexplicable need to comfort him. She held up a hand and he stepped over, taking her fingers in his, hesitantly. It was strange how she had not held these hands in years, yet the strong, calloused fingers seemed so familiar. "Thank you, for everything you did for me."

Then the reality of the situation suddenly hit home with full force. She had been shot and it was no accident. If he hadn't been there to help her, she would be dead, her blood seeping out onto the snow until someone eventually found her body. A cold wind seemed to blow through her, wrapping her in frigid gales of fear. His voice sounded very far away.

"Jackie? Are you all right?"

Roman's eyes melted into hers, bringing her back. There was the slightest tremor on his lips as he bent down and held his cheek to her hand. The touch seemed to set off an electric current through her body and she knew what she had to do. After drawing in a deep, shuddering breath, she told him everything.

He listened without speaking, standing motionless until she was through.

"So you see why we can't go to the police yet. I know I've been an idiot, Roman. I'm sorry for getting you involved. I have no right." Especially after the things she said.

He shook his head as if to clear it for a moment and took a deep breath. "Don't apologize, Jackie. One way or another, we're going to get you out of this mess." He leaned close and kissed her cheek, wrapping her in a faint scent of musk. He whispered the words in her ear that seemed to flow throughout her body in a tide of comfort. "I promise."

The next morning Roman waited patiently while Skip checked Jackie out of the hospital. He tried to stretch out the kink in his back from sleeping in a chair in the waiting area. After what she had told him, there was no way he was leaving her alone. In spite of his concern, he smiled at the chagrined look on her face at having to be pushed out in a wheelchair.

"Hospital policy," Skip reminded her cheerfully, as they got into the van and drove back to the airstrip where he'd left the de Havilland. Once they were aboard, Roman got a better look at her.

Face pale, eyes shadowed, Jackie moved only a little tentatively as she buckled her seat belt. He mulled over her revelation again, wondering what she intended to tell the police. In spite of the worry, he felt an odd sense of elation; she'd confided in him, trusted him, and it made him feel ten feet tall. If he could not share his love with her, he could at least keep her safe. It would have to be enough.

The river of people needing hopper flights to their various Winterfest accommodations had lessened, or been snapped up by the other aviation companies, so Wayne gave him permission to help with the activities at the lodge. He was happy to have an excuse to keep close to Jackie, but he couldn't help the fear that overtook him. What if he couldn't protect her? What if she died too?

Lord, don't let me fail her.

When they disembarked, there were only two snowmobiles waiting. Roman climbed on one. Strapping on an overstuffed backpack, Skip climbed on the other. After an awkward moment, Jackie slid onto the seat behind Roman on his snowmobile.

He tried not to react when her good arm slid around his waist and tightened as the motor gunned to life. She pressed her face into his shoulders as they made their way along. He concentrated on avoiding as many of the bumps as he could, to keep from jarring her shoulder.

At the lodge the sculptors had already begun to transform the big blocks of snow into crystalline flowers, horses and totems. Skip excused himself and trotted off toward the throng. Roman escorted Jackie into the lodge, which was warmed by a massive fire and filled with people.

The village public safety officer was waiting, amid a swarm of people with coffee mugs in their hands. Officer Tom Brady's round cheeks and thick brows brought back a series of bad memories. He'd been the one to investigate the accident two years ago, before the Alaska state trooper had arrived to take over.

Roman saw Jackie tense. He wondered if she too remembered the officer, or if it was the current situation that affected her. After a deep breath, she held her chin up and followed the stout official to a relatively quiet corner. Roman grabbed a cup of coffee and sat down out of earshot. The officer spoke to her for what seemed a very long while and then gestured for Roman to join them.

Brady got right to the point. "Hello, Roman. What happened last night?"

Roman recounted the shooting as best he could.

The officer nodded. "I got that much from her. Do you have any idea why someone might be interested in shooting Ms. Swann?"

Roman blinked. Had Jackie told Brady about the break-in at her cabin? She turned a beseeching look on Roman, with eyes that tore at his heart. *Trust me,* they seemed to say. He cleared his throat and stuck to the bare-bones truth. "I don't know anybody who'd want to hurt Jackie."

Brady scratched his neck with a pencil. "Okay. Looks like one of those crazy things that happens from time to time. I'll take a cruise out along the top of the bluff, but I don't expect to find anything. I'd stay out of the woods at night, if I were you, Ms. Swann. Or take this big guy with you, just in case." Brady bobbed a chin at Roman.

Jackie's cheeks colored, but she said nothing as the officer left.

Roman noticed that her hands were shaking, her fingers laced together tightly on her lap.

She looked so lost and scared that Roman couldn't stand it. He took her hand and moved until their knees touched.

Tears pooled in her eyes. "Oh, Roman. I think I made a mistake, a big mistake, and I don't know how to fix it."

He considered his words carefully. "I know what that feels like—to make a mistake that turns your life upside down."

Jackie sighed. "You've been so good to me through all this. Why?"

"Old times sake."

She smiled. "We had some great times, didn't we?"

His breath caught at the gentle look on her face. "The best times of my life were spent with you."

She looked at him and it was as if she could see right down into the very bottom of his soul. Could she face the sorrow there? The terrible regret for what he had done to them all? A tear slid down her face and he reached out a finger and traced its salty path down her smooth cheek. She closed her eyes. With a small shudder she opened them again, a mask of control falling over her features.

"I'm a little tired. I'm going to go lie down so I can help with the sculpture competition later."

"Don't worry about it. You rest. I can take care of everything."

She smiled in spite of the tears. "Thanks, but you know I'm going to help anyway."

He laughed. "Yes, I do."

NINE

He sat there long after Jackie had left, trying to make sense of his own actions. He wondered if Jackie regretted confiding in him. It would have been easier if she hadn't. The sight of her distress broke open the barricades around his heart he'd painstakingly spent two years building. He was supposed to be staying away from her, far away, but now he felt the urge to keep her in his sights every minute.

June bustled in, steadying a towering pile of boxes, and he rushed to assist her.

She gave him a grateful smile. "Where is Fallon? We've got twenty pounds of potatoes to peel and she's supposed to be on kitchen duty. Go find her, will you?"

He nodded and made for the back corner of the main lodge, toward Fallon's room, running into Lloyd a few feet from Fallon's doorway. He heard the sound of crying from her bedroom.

Lloyd smiled and moved to pass by, but Roman shot out an arm to bar the way.

"What's going on?"

Lloyd gave him a blank look. "Going on? Nothing, I'd say. On my way to the snow-sculpture deal."

"Why is Fallon crying?"

He blinked. "How would I know that?"

Roman's voice was hard. "Because you were in there with her. I suggest you explain to me right now why she is upset, Mr. Lloyd."

Lloyd looked uneasy for a moment before he broke into another smile. "I happened to be going that way and I heard her sniffling. I knocked on the door to check on things and found her crying."

"About what?"

He shrugged. "You know the fickle ways of the teenager. I'm not sure what her dilemma is. I talked with her for a while and then excused myself."

"Is that what she's going to tell me?"

"Absolutely. Look, I understand your protectiveness. I've got a teenage niece, and I'd be concerned about some old geezer my age sniffing around. Believe me, there's nothing sinister going on here. I was just lending a sympathetic ear, that's all."

Roman lowered his arm, and Lloyd continued on toward the dining hall. Roman waited until he was out of sight before he knocked on Fallon's door.

"It's Roman. Can I come in?"

There was a scuffling sound before she answered. "Okay."

Her face was blotchy, eyes swollen. She sat on the bed with her arms folded, looking very small in her oversize sweatshirt. The room was cluttered with books, clothes draped over every available surface, littered with magazines featuring bands he'd never heard of.

"Your mom sent me to look for you." Roman tilted his head at the door. "That guy bothering you?"

"Who? Mr. Lloyd? Nah. He's the only one around here who listens to me."

Roman moved a pile of scarves and sat on a beanbag opposite the bed. "I'm listening. What's bugging you?"

She blew her nose. "Nothing."

"I don't think people cry over nothing."

She gave him a sullen shrug.

He took a deep breath. "Fallon, what did you mean at the hospital when you said it was your fault Danny was killed?"

Her eyes widened for a moment, but she kept her lips firmly pressed together and gave him another shrug.

"Well, I just wanted to say, I want you to know that it wasn't anybody's fault but mine, see? You shouldn't feel responsible just because you may have had some feelings for him, okay?"

Her face turned a rosy pink. "It's not that. Besides, he thought of me as a little sister. That's why he agreed to…" She trailed off.

"Agreed to what?"

"Never mind. It doesn't matter anyway." She began to pile the books on the bed into a stack.

"Maybe it does matter, Fallon. Obviously you've given it a lot of thought. What did you ask Danny to do for you?"

She looked dangerously close to bursting into tears. "I said, never mind. I shouldn't have brought it up, anyway. Mom wants me in the kitchen, right?"

"Yeah. Potato-peeling duty."

She jumped off the bed and wiped her nose with her sleeve. "Figures."

Roman noticed a photo on the bedspread and picked it up. It was a woman, vaguely familiar, though he could not identify her. "Who's this?"

Fallon snatched the photo out of his hands, her face stricken. She shoved it into the pocket of her jeans. "No one. I've got to go."

No one? He turned the thought around in his mind as he closed the door softly.

Jackie paced the cabin floor until she could stand it no longer. If she could just figure out what exactly had happened at Dr. Reynolds's office. She knew there must be claims made under the names of Reynolds's patients. That much was clear from the desperate lengths someone had gone through to find the thumb drive. How did Dr. Reynolds funnel the money back to his own pockets?

It would have been easy to falsify insurance claims that would pay directly back to his office. Most patients had no access to their electronic files, so they'd never know about his treachery. They would be blissfully unaware until they applied for a job or were denied insurance because of the mysterious conditions on their charts. She imagined a poor, unsuspecting victim trying to get into the fire service, sidelined by a fictitious heart murmur, or a bus driver who was denied a position for a similar reason. Folks being turned down for life insurance because of conditions they would never experience.

The whole business was complicated, sophisticated. Asia thought patients were affected in other offices as well. In their region alone Asia had found suspicious claims from two cardiology offices in southern California and one in Nevada. The evidence was too deeply buried, filtered through an arsenal of insurance companies and accounting firms. She knew she couldn't figure it out on her own. She needed to keep the thumb drive safe until Asia arrived with her conclusions. Would Jackie be alive long enough to see it through? She shivered. *Roman is watching out for you, Jackie.* The thought brought her a level of comfort she would not have imagined.

Walking to the window, she saw the crowd milling about the sculptors, who had a scant hour left to finish their masterpieces. She felt so lonely looking at the happy throng, so far away from the happiness out there. The loss of her brother rose fresh inside her. It had been a mistake to come to Alaska.

Roman's words came back to her.

I know what that feels like—to make a mistake that turns your life upside down.

She hated the pain that had nestled in his eyes and robbed him of the roguish quality that had always appealed to her. She knew she should forgive. The words from Isaiah floated into her mind like the snowflakes that had begun to fall.

"Though your sins are as scarlet, they will be as white as snow."

Forgiveness was a precious gift, the Lord's way of loving His children. But she could not give it to Roman. She could not offer him her absolution for the blood on his hands, her brother's blood. It made her feel even more guilty for confiding her problems in him.

She pulled on a jacket and headed out into the snow.

The noise and confusion of the festivalgoers was a welcome distraction. There would only be a little daylight left before the competition came to a close. The snow was falling harder now and the temperature seemed to plunge with every second. An earlier radio broadcast had issued a winter storm warning, but the strong wind that buffeted the festival crowd hinted at a full-fledged blizzard.

In spite of the elements, the sculptors, bundled to the neck, continued to put the finishing touches on their creations. Jackie gazed in wonder at an enormous carving of a whale that seemed to ride on a wave of snow. People took pictures and held mugs of June's hot cocoa in their gloved hands. Two young blond women with down jackets and tight jeans stood nearby chatting.

A hand touched Jackie's arm, startling her. She turned to find Mick grinning at her. "How's the shoulder?"

"Sore, but okay. I didn't think I'd see you today."

"Skip called. Said he needed more help." He hefted a

shovel as if it was a free weight. "Good for the muscles." He turned to move a wooden board out of the way of a boy pulling a toboggan.

Mick tried to speak to her again, but the rising wind drowned him out until he called into her ear. "Come on. I need to talk to you."

She allowed him to guide her into the lodge, where Skip spoke worriedly into a cell phone.

Mick moved to a corner near the fireplace. "I've heard from Asia. She's uncovered some more info."

Jackie felt a jolt of excitement. "Excellent. Can we go to Health and Human Services now? Or the police?"

"She's still trying to connect the dots."

Jackie sighed. "I know. I've been trying, too. I wish my brother was still alive. He had such a mind for numbers, and he was a computer whiz."

Mick huffed. "My brother wouldn't cross the street to help me in any way."

"Not close?"

Mick shrugged. "Things sort of fell apart between us when my parents divorced. My dad was my hero. Still is, even though he died two years ago."

"I'm sorry."

"It happens. I went crazy, partying, moving from place to place and job to job. I still can't stand to be penned in. I'm the black sheep in the family." He grinned. "Fortunately, I'm a really handsome sheep."

She laughed. "Lucky for the lady sheep. So Asia is okay, then? How come she hasn't contacted me? Maybe I'm not getting all my e-mails."

A bulky figure approached. "Not getting your e-mails, young lady? I heard you had a break-in. Did the burglar take your computer?" Lloyd smiled at them and held his hands to the fire.

Jackie started. "No…"

Mick gave Lloyd an annoyed look. "Hey, man. Eavesdropping is rude, you know?"

"My apologies. Occupational hazard." Lloyd moved away.

Mick spoke quietly. "Nosy guy. Who is he? Tourist?"

Jackie shook her head. "I don't think so. He's been asking questions about me and my background. He told us he's a reporter for a magazine, but I did some online snooping and found out he was lying."

Mick nodded thoughtfully. "Maybe he took a shot at you, too."

Jackie inhaled sharply. Had he been in the crowd that found her? "But why try to kill me if he's after the files on the thumb drive?"

Mick looked intently at Lloyd, who had engaged one of the blond ladies in conversation.

"Could be he's supposed to get the thumb drive and then take care of any loose ends."

She felt as if she'd had ice water injected into her veins. Legs shaking, she sank down onto a leather-covered bench.

He sat next to her.

"It's just all too much. I wonder if it's time to go to the police. Roman thinks…"

Mick shook his head. "I suggested to Asia that we should contact the Alaska police, but she said we had to wait."

"Why?"

He sighed. "Because the three of us had access to confidential patient records and Reynolds can deny everything—make it look like you and Asia are dirty, and me too, for that matter."

She groaned and pressed her hands to her temples, which had begun to throb. "I was afraid of that. If things get any worse, we may not have any choice but to involve the police."

He nodded grimly. "Are you sure you're safe at the lodge? You can come bunk in my cabin. There are plenty of rooms."

She cast a glance at Roman, who was refilling coffeepots across the room. "I'm okay here."

Mick followed her gaze. "With that guy? He has done a real lousy job of keeping you safe, so far."

That's because I haven't let him get close enough. The look in his eyes when he had found her shot spoke volumes. He'd sacrifice his own life for hers. The thought warmed a place deep inside that had lain cold for two long years. *It's penance for Danny. He's looking after you out of guilt, pure and simple.* She would not let him ease his conscience so easily.

Rekindling her resolve, she straightened. "Roman's not a part of my life anymore."

"You sure about that? Seems like you two were thick."

"That was a long time ago." She watched Roman, his dark eyes glimmering in the firelight. "A lifetime ago."

TEN

The weather continued to worsen. Snow rattled against the windows and Mick added logs to the fire. Dax barreled through the door, his hat coated with a thin crust of ice. He stamped to the fire and warmed himself for a moment before he joined them. "Storm's kicking up." He eyed Mick. "You can't get back to your cabin tonight. June said staff and guests can sleep on the floor in here. Got some cots in the storage room."

Mick shook his head. "No, no. I can make my way back."

Dax's weathered face remained unchanged. "Best to stay here."

Mick started to answer. At a look from Dax, he sighed. "So much for my luxury vacation."

"Might need to move the folks outside in here if things get much worse."

"Are we going to lose power?"

Dax snorted. "We're not on the grid out here. Everything's on generators anyway."

Mick shook his head. "I should have known that."

Jackie chuckled. "Too long in the city. I forget too. I'd better go ask Skip if he needs to put any of the women in my cabin."

Mick followed Dax into the kitchen, and Jackie headed for the small office where she knew she'd find Skip. Roman stopped her.

"How's the shoulder?"

"Okay. Nothing that will keep me down for long." She intended to brush by him when she remembered Mick's comment. "I wanted to ask you something, about the shooting."

He gave her a nod of encouragement.

"When you found me, was anybody with you?"

"No. I got to you first. After a while, people started to gather."

"What people?"

Roman looked up at the ceiling. "I've been going over and over that, as a matter of fact. Skip and Fallon were there. One of the sculptors and the two blond women. And Lloyd."

"Did Lloyd arrive with the rest of the group?"

He thought a moment. "Couple minutes behind, I think. Why? Are you suggesting he was the shooter?"

A tense knot settled in the pit of her stomach. "I don't know. I don't trust him, that's for sure. He doesn't write for *Adventure Road*, the magazine name he gave me. Mick thinks he might work for the crime ring that Reynolds sells his info to."

Roman frowned. "Does Mick know something he's not telling?"

"No. He wants this solved just as much as we do." She tried to move away, but he inched closer. The smell of wood smoke clung to him and she had the strong urge to brush away the hair that lay across his face. "Don't worry about Mick. He's a good guy."

"I worry about anyone who might get you deeper into trouble."

"It's not your job to worry about me anymore, Roman. You were a good sport to listen to my problems but I need to handle them on my own."

"I'll always worry about you. You're not doing real well on your own so far. Someone's got to look out for you."

She saw the old cockiness in his face, the confidence that had attracted her like a moth to a flame. He was the same Roman she'd left behind, the man who had killed her brother. The words spilled out before she could stop them. "Like you looked out for Danny?"

He stepped back as if she'd slapped him. At that moment she wanted more than anything to erase what she'd just said.

"I'm sorry." She forced out a breath. "I've been steeped in anger so long. I'm sorry."

He looked at the floor. "No big deal."

"Yes it is." She grabbed his hand. "I never thought until I came back here how things were for you. Oh, Roman. We had such plans, didn't we? You were going to buy a plane and we'd run our little company together."

A ghost of a smile crossed his face. "Yeah. Alaskan Adventure Air. A great dream, wasn't it?" His smile dimmed.

"Your mother made us a logo and everything." A thought occurred to her. "How is your mother? How did she…handle it all?"

"She disappeared."

Jackie gasped. "What?"

"Oh, not like that. She withdrew. I don't know if it was the shame of having a son who killed someone or the fear of hearing people blame me, but she quit her activities and became kind of a hermit. She's still that way. I have to strong-arm her even to get her to come out to dinner with me."

She wrapped him in a hug. "I'm so sorry, Roman."

She wanted to press the awful grief out of him. His arms tightened around her for a moment and then his lips brushed her neck before he pulled away.

"Me too," he whispered before he left.

She watched him go. Her breathing was unsteady as she continued down the hallway to find Skip. She'd never even thought about Roman's mother. Jackie's own callousness shocked her. Maybe the anger had finally twisted her soul into something dark and cruel.

When she approached the open door, she heard Skip's voice, tinged with anger as he spoke on the phone.

"That wasn't part of our deal."

Deal? The intensity in his words made her think this was not routine lodge business. She remembered the money he'd dropped in town. She cleared her throat to let him know of her approach, but his irate conversation continued.

"It isn't right. You can't blackmail us forever. We don't have that kind of money."

Jackie stopped, uneasy to be privy to what was clearly a painful conversation. She decided to retreat and take up the matter with Skip later. Turning around, she yelped to see Byron Lloyd a few steps behind her.

He raised a thick eyebrow. "Sounds like the boss is into something."

She aimed a glare at him. "Something we're not meant to overhear."

"Yup," he said, dark eyes glittering. "Secrets are like that."

A few hours later Roman listened to the National Weather Radio upgrade the warning from severe winter storm to blizzard. He called Wayne.

"Looks like I'm going to be here for a while."

"Might as well be. No flying, anyway."

"Yeah."

Wayne must have heard a strange tone in Roman's voice. "What's going on over there? Figure out anything on that shooting? Jackie okay?"

"Fine, stubborn as always."

Wayne laughed. "Imagine. So what did the cops say?"

Roman smiled at the eager tone in his friend's voice. "Nothing to say. Just one of those weird things."

"Hmm, I don't buy it. Watch your back, Roman," he said before hanging up.

I will, he thought, *and Jackie's too.*

Her words cut as deftly as his hunting knife.

Like you looked out for Danny?

He wanted to immerse himself in the memory of that awful day, to relive every tiny detail until he could finally make sense of what had happened and put it to rest, but a haze of confused memory still swirled in his head like the driving snow outside. He wasn't sure remembering would help anymore. Maybe the amnesia was a blessing.

A bustle of activity pulled him from his reverie. Skip was issuing orders, his face grim.

"Looks like we're going to have to ride out this blizzard. Winds are too high to fly or drive anyone out. All the guests camped outside will have to be moved in here. Dax, let's get these tables pushed to the side of the room. Roman and Mick, can you assist folks to move their gear and such inside?" He scanned the room.

"I can help June," Jackie offered. "And you can bunk people in my cabin."

He gave her a relieved smile. "I appreciate it, Jackie. Mr. Lloyd offered to give up his place too."

Roman looked for Lloyd in the dining hall, but did not find him. He didn't see Fallon either, which made him uncomfortable. He tried to catch Jackie's eye to have her check on Fallon, but she had already disappeared into the kitchen. Without waiting for Mick, Roman put on his jacket and stepped into the storm.

The thirty-mile-per-hour winds had already forced piles of snow to half cover the snow sculptures. It was a good thing Skip had hurriedly taken pictures and urged the judges to take a close look. Under the line of white-covered trees the campers fought the wind and freezing chill to pack their gear as best they could. It was impossible to take the tents down, but Roman helped roll up sleeping bags and heft backpacks filled with belongings into the lodge. All told, there were close to thirty visitors who would need a place to sleep. He caught sight of Mick, arms full of gear, leading the two young blond ladies toward Jackie's cabin.

Inside, the dining lodge was rapidly filling with neatly unrolled sleeping bags.

A red-cheeked man with a limp mustache caught Roman by the arm. "How bad? Will we be stuck here for long? What if the food runs out?"

Roman held up a hand. "It'll be okay. We get these blizzards from time to time." He surveyed the man's bright Gore-Tex jacket. "New here?"

The man groaned. "I wanted to go to Hawaii, but the wife insisted on having a wilderness adventure. Camping in the snow? How did I let myself get talked into this? Do you know how much I paid for that tent?"

Roman turned away before he chuckled aloud. Alaska was more than a destination; it was a state of mind. Fierce independence, a calm acceptance of the extreme elements God drew together in one massive state, a place of self-reliant, unconventional individuals.

He thought of Jackie and how she had always fit perfectly into the wild landscape, even though she was not a native Alaskan. She was normally unshakable; he'd seen her help dig a family out of a cabin that had collapsed under the weight of a heavy load of ice without flinching. But she was different now; there was an uncertainty about her that told him the events in San Francisco had frightened her badly, and the danger followed her here. The shooter was out in that wild Alaskan blizzard. An ugly thought made his gut twist. Was the person who wanted Jackie dead tucked safely into the lodge waiting for a chance to try again?

Mick came in, stomping the clumps of snow from his boots.

Roman sauntered over. "Find a place to bunk?"

Mick looked startled. "Yeah, got a cot over near the fire. I still think I could have made it back to my cabin. How long you figure the storm will last?"

"Hard to say." Roman shoved his hands into his pockets. "So, you work with Jackie in San Francisco?"

Mick nodded.

"She's in the front office. You do that kind of thing, too?"

"No. I fix the imaging machines." He eyed Roman. "That's the equipment that allows the doctor to take pictures of the heart, et cetera."

I know what it is, Roman wanted to snap. Instead he forced a smile. "Interesting work?"

"You bet. Lets me travel and all. I service offices up and down the coast. But my girl works at Jackie's office so I spend a lot of time there." He eyed Roman. "You get out of Alaska much?"

Roman flushed. "Not often. I visited San Francisco once and saw the office. What's the doctor's name again?"

Mick gave Roman a close look. "Reynolds. I'm sure you could get that info from a quick Google search, so why the twenty questions? You worried she's two-timing you?"

Roman's fists clenched. "Just being neighborly. We do that here in Alaska."

"Uh-huh. Well, if you want any more information, why don't you ask Jackie? If she'll talk to you." Mick turned away.

It took all Roman's self-control not to knock Mick to the floor. He tried to slow the angry hammering of his heart. The prying had given him an idea.

ELEVEN

Jackie helped June finish the dishes and put batches of dried cranberry and white-chocolate cookies into the oven for late-night snackers. June took a moment to wipe her hands on her apron and survey the kitchen. Her eyes were heavily shadowed, face deeply wrinkled. She sighed.

"Are you okay, June?"

"What? Oh, sure. We've weathered plenty of blizzards since we started this place."

"That's not what I meant. You look tired and...sort of stressed."

June put her hands to her cheeks. "Do I? Winterfest is a busy time."

"You thrive on busy, June. You look worried about something else. Is there anything I can help with?"

She gave Jackie a tender smile. "No, sweetie. I guess it's been harder than usual the last couple of years."

"Can you hire some staff? You used to have a housekeeper, didn't you?"

June waved a hand. "Don't need a housekeeper. I've got plenty of energy and a daughter to help out, when she chooses to, anyway." She grimaced. "Teenagers are hard work. You just never know quite what to do with them."

Jackie chuckled. "I think my father would agree. I heard you called him."

June nodded. "Your arrival put it into my head. I hadn't spoken to him in quite a while. Skip used to call him all the time until…" She pressed her lips together. "I'm sorry. I didn't mean to bring it up."

"It's okay." Jackie was surprised to find that she really meant it. "I've been thinking a lot about Danny since I arrived."

A faraway look crossed June's face. "He was a daredevil, for sure, but so good-hearted. He'd do anything for anyone, wouldn't he?"

Jackie nodded. "Yes, he would. Danny was an amazing person, and it's good to talk about him. He loved it here. He wanted to learn to work on the pipeline like Dad so he could live here permanently." She shook her head. "I guess I've spent so much time trying to forget about the accident, I've shut out the good times too. Coming here has brought it all up again."

June twisted a dish towel in her hands. "I think maybe I shouldn't have called your father. I felt this overwhelming desire to talk to him, but he didn't seem very comfortable talking to me. I think my call dredged up some bad feelings."

"We had so many wonderful times here, so many great memories, but it seems like that all got erased once Danny died. My father hasn't accepted it yet. I don't know if he ever will."

"Have you?" June looked at her with a mixture of pity and some unfathomable emotion. "Have you accepted your brother's death?"

The question startled her. "I, I thought I had until…"

June spoke softly. "Until you saw Roman again?"

She nodded.

"It's been terrible on him too, you know. Tore him apart and his mother. He's had to face so much that you can't imagine."

Jackie's heart squeezed painfully in her chest. "I think I can imagine."

"Can you? To live every day knowing that someone died

because of you? To have no one believe your version of the accident? To not be able to clearly remember exactly what did happen? Can you imagine what that's like?" June moved closer, her eyes filled with tears, and took Jackie's hand, squeezing her fingers. "Oh, Jackie. If only we could erase it, that one decision, we would in a heartbeat."

Jackie felt as if she'd just stepped off a riverbank into a bottomless current. "What decision?"

Abruptly June let go and hurried toward the door. "Nothing. I'm babbling. Must be more tired than I thought. I've got to go see about things. Skip will need help organizing people's baggage."

What decision did June regret so deeply?

Roman's face filled her mind again. What would it feel like to shoulder so heavy a burden? To lose your friend, and your love in one moment?

Restlessness drove her out of the kitchen. Jackie found a quiet corner and called her father. She was pleased that he sounded robust and eager to talk.

"Why didn't you tell me you were going to Delucchi's?"

"It was kind of a spur-of-the-moment thing. I didn't plan it out, really."

"June told me Roman still works around there. Have you seen him?"

"Yes. He flew me from the airport to the lodge." She didn't mention the shooting incident and the fact that he'd taken her to the hospital.

"I guess you didn't know."

"I should have figured he'd be working for a transport service."

"You stay away from him, do you hear me?"

The anger in his words seemed to strike at her. "Dad, it was a long time ago."

"I don't care. He killed your brother. Never forget that."

"I won't forget it." She wished that she could have her old father back. The one who didn't have anger running through his veins like a swiftly moving poison. She thought of Roman and the agony in his eyes. Despite what her father might think, Roman had been greatly damaged by the accident too.

"Dad, you know, I really think Roman is sorry—"

She didn't get a chance to finish.

"He should be sorry. He should be sorry for the rest of his life. I will never forgive him and neither should you."

She realized that the moment she'd lost her brother, she'd lost her father too. It stoked the anger inside her, which had begun, for the briefest of moments, to wane. Now it flared again. Her father was right. They'd all been ruined by Roman's carelessness.

She talked for a short while longer before they both said good-night. As she hung up, Jackie felt grateful for the reminder. *Stay away from Roman.* She flashed on his warm, hazel eyes and the feel of his strong arms lifting her out of the snow.

Far, far away.

Though Wayne seemed eager to loan Roman his laptop, Roman could hear a slight hesitation in his voice over the phone.

"I'll have Jimmy snowmobile it to you this morning if he can get through. I agree with you that the burglary and shooting are probably related and both have something to do with Dr. Reynolds."

"But?"

"But I'm wondering if this is going to open up a road that you don't want to go down again."

Roman sighed. "She's in danger, more than she will admit to. I don't have much of a choice."

"Sure you do. Leave it alone. Let Jackie and Mick and whoever else is involved sort it out. I'm not sure it's a good idea for you to get mixed up with her again."

"I'm not ."

"I mean this in the most caring way—you're kidding yourself."

"Look, Wayne. I want to be sure she's safe, that's all."

"Why?"

"Why?"

"Yeah, why? Because you're torn up with guilt about Danny? Or because you still love her?"

Roman felt warm. "None of the above."

He heard Wayne exhale slowly. "Roman, I saw how long it took you to reconstruct the pieces of your life after the accident. I'd hate to watch you put your heart out there for Jackie and have it broken again. She made it clear how she felt about you when she left the last time."

"I just want to poke around a little."

"Okay, but don't say I didn't try to hammer some sense into that big head of yours."

Roman disconnected. Wayne was right. Jackie had made it painfully clear how she felt when she'd left Alaska the last time.

I'll never forgive you.

Was he drawing deeper into her problems out of guilt?

Or love?

Just before midnight, Roman lay on his cot, trying to screen out the snoring from the man on the sleeping bag next to him. It was cold in the dining hall. The generator kept the heat functioning, but the temperature outside had dropped to nearly twenty below. Wind still shook the cabin in angry gusts. Roman decided to find a spot away from the sleeping guests and fire up the borrowed laptop.

As he fumbled for his shoes underneath his cot, he became aware of a soft noise from the far end of the room. He sank back down to listen. It was the sound of rustling clothing followed by the noise of a zipper. Someone preparing to head to the bathroom down the hall? The room was cold, but not that cold.

He listened for a few more moments until he heard the clunk of shoes being fished out from under a cot. Who would be getting dressed now? Preparing to go where? With a blizzard howling, the only sane choice was to ride it out inside.

Roman froze, trying to decipher the noises. A figure on that far end of the room was standing now, moving slowly in the direction of the hallway. With only the faintest light of the exit sign showing, Roman could not make out if the figure was male or female. Whoever it was headed slowly down the hallway. He waited until the person had rounded the corner before he eased out of his cot. Slipping on shoes, he followed, sticking to the shadowed periphery of the hallway.

Rounding the corner, Roman saw the figure pause, as if listening for something, and then continue on toward the exit door at the end of the hallway.

Exit? There was no place to go except out into the blinding storm. Roman thought about Jackie and the break-ins at her cabin, the bullet that could have taken her life. Could this bundled figure be heading for her, mistakenly thinking she was sleeping in the cabin?

He knew he could shout and get the attention of the guests staying in the dining room. More than anything, he wanted to know what this person was after and to make sure Jackie was safe from the wandering stranger.

Three feet more and the figure would be at the door. Roman held his breath, easing along as silently as he could. A tiny squeak from behind made him stop dead. Was someone else following? He turned and scanned the dark space, but saw nothing in the blackness. His imagination was in overdrive. He returned his attention to the person, who reached out for the door handle.

Roman readied himself and took two steps closer. "Stop right there."

The figure whirled around and aimed a punch. Anticipating

the blow made Roman duck, but the fist caught him on the cheekbone. He staggered back a step before hurling himself at his assailant.

There was a shout from behind him, but Roman was too caught up to notice. He punched the guy under the chin and they both toppled over, knocking over a coatrack with a deafening crash. The person wormed out of Roman's grasp by sliding out of his jacket. He made it to the door, where Roman brought him down again. They rolled and smashed into the walls, until Roman felt a pair of hands on his shoulders, dragging him upward.

TWELVE

Running feet thundered down the hallway and a crash split the night along with a shout. Jackie jerked upright in her sleeping bag. After a second of uncertainty, she disentangled herself and took off at a run. She joined a few others, clumsy with sleep, making their way quickly toward the noise.

Someone snapped on a light, and she saw two men rolling on the floor. One shed his jacket in an effort to escape. It was Mick, his face a mixture of anger and surprise. Roman grabbed him by the shirt and they went over again, fists flying.

"Stop!" She didn't realize she'd cried it aloud. The word didn't penetrate, as the men continued to go after each other.

Lloyd pushed through the group and grabbed Roman by his shoulders. Skip did the same with Mick. They both stood, panting, eyeing each other with venom.

"What is going on here?" Skip demanded.

Roman shook loose from Lloyd's grip. "I heard someone prowling around. I thought he was up to no good."

Skip looked at Mick, his eyebrows raised in a question.

He huffed. "I couldn't sleep with that snoring. Sounds like a chain saw, so I decided to go back to the hunting cabin."

Jackie gaped. "Mick, there's a blizzard out there. You can't travel in this."

"I know how to take care of myself," he snapped, pulling away from Skip and straightening. "No need for Paul Bunyan here to attack me."

Roman grunted. "I didn't attack you. I told you to stop and you threw a punch at me."

"Instinct. You should have explained yourself."

Roman glared. "I don't have to explain myself. Any idiot knows you can't make it back to your cabin in this weather."

Mick grabbed his jacket from the floor. "Maybe *you* can't."

"I'm not going to let you get yourself stuck in the snow."

"Why do you care?"

Roman's voice swelled to a roar. "Because Skip and I are the ones that are going to have to go out and chip your frozen carcass out of the ice."

As Mick struggled to pull on his jacket, a tattoo on his forearm shone eerily in the lamplight. "Really sorry, man, but I've got to get to my cabin." His black eyes still flashed with anger. "Air's just too thick in here." He reached out for the door again and Roman grabbed his arm.

"You try to get back to that hunting cabin and you'll die of hypothermia."

Mick tried again to leave but Roman held his arm.

Jackie took a step forward. "Mick, listen to Roman. He's right."

Mick twisted away.

Lloyd cleared his throat. "Maybe I can offer a solution. My cabin has three men in it now, but it sleeps four easily. Why don't you head over there? Here's a little insurance policy for you." He held up two yellow bits of foam, beaming. "Earplugs. I never travel without them. The ex-wife snored like a runaway freight train."

Mick grudgingly followed Skip out into the swirling snow toward Lloyd's cabin. The sleepy onlookers wandered back to their cots. Jackie watched a trickle of blood snake down Roman's face from a small cut on his cheek. She took his hand. "Come on."

He looked startled, but didn't resist. "Where?"

"For some first aid." She led him to the kitchen. "Sit down."

"I'm fine."

"Sit anyway."

He sat in a kitchen chair and she fetched a clean towel and a bottle of antiseptic. She pushed away the hair that hung across his forehead and dabbed gently at his bloodied cheek. He sat very still and she tried not to notice the feel of his muscled shoulder where she held on with one hand.

Being so close to him, his mouth inches from hers, made her head swim. An impulse seized hold of her, to rub her cheek against his strong jaw, to bury her face under the slightly stubbled chin and feel the pulse beating in his throat. She blinked and cleared her throat. "You didn't need to hit him."

"He hit me first."

She smiled at the sullen-little-boy frown on Roman's face. "Well, that changes everything."

"I thought he was a prowler, for one, and anyway you know I'm right. He'd die quick out there."

"I know. You are right. Mick is a good guy, he's just out of his element here and he's stubborn." She smiled. "Asia says that's his middle name."

"I still think it's strange that she didn't she come with him to Alaska. Why would a guy leave her behind, especially when she's in trouble?"

Jackie tried to move away, but he grabbed her hand and kept her there, pulled close to his side.

She knew that Roman wasn't thinking about Mick and Asia. Her stomach fluttered and she spoke hurriedly. "It was Asia's decision. She's going to fly out here in a few days."

Roman's eyes seemed to see right into her heart. "Doesn't seem right for a guy to leave his girlfriend. If he loves her, he should stand by her. If she'll let him."

"It's not what you think."

"What is it then?"

She aimed for a bright tone. "Nothing at all. Asia will be here soon and you'll see that I'm right." She filled a towel with ice cubes and pressed it to his cheek.

His look changed as he stared at her. "I guess I've been wrong before. About pretty much everything."

The impulse was so strong she didn't have time to control it before she leaned down and brushed her lips against his un-injured cheekbone. "Thank you," she whispered. "For keeping Mick safe in spite of himself."

She heard his sharp intake of breath and left quickly, not daring to meet his eyes.

Roman was up, digging out the plane before most of the guests awakened to take in the aftermath of the blizzard. He'd cleared off the wings and was working on the landing strip when he saw Mick zoom away on the snowmobile. He'd managed to make it through the night in Lloyd's cabin.

When the area was ready for takeoff he returned to the lodge, toward the enticing smell of pancakes and bacon.

Skip took a break from clearing the piles of snow under the windows and joined Roman. He peered up at the clear sky. "Good storm."

"Yeah. Everyone seemed to survive it okay." He eyed the mounds of white where the sculptures had been. "Too bad about the artwork."

"Judges saw enough to make a decision. Come on. I'm an-nouncing it over breakfast."

Roman filled a plate and sat in a chair to eat, leaving the benches for the crowd. He noticed Jackie, but Lloyd was missing from the group.

When he finished eating, Roman took his plate to the

kitchen. He gave June a kiss on the cheek. "Thanks for breakfast, Mrs. D. I've got to go earn some money now."

"Plane okay?"

"Sure." He gave her a smile. "Cold seats, but I'll be fine."

She looked closely at his bruised cheek. "That friend of Jackie's give you the shiner? Skip told me about the scuffle. I guess I was so tired I slept right through it."

"I'm glad we didn't wake you. I think Fallon slept through it too." He looked around and stuck his head into the dining room for a moment. "Where is she?"

"Sleeping late, probably. She only seems interested in sleeping and eating these days."

"Sounds like a typical teen to me." He said good-bye and headed outside. Jackie avoided looking at him as he passed by. He'd made her promise to stay inside while he was gone. He remembered the kiss when she'd thanked him for keeping Mick safe. For a guy who had a girlfriend back home, Mick was spending plenty of time with Jackie. He pushed through the snow and started the engines to warm the plane. It felt good to be back in control again, away from Jackie and all the feelings she brought to life.

After he'd delivered the outgoing passengers to the airport, Roman returned to Wayne's Aviation to wait for another guest, turning on the borrowed laptop to make use of the time. He was glad he'd taken the community college classes several years back. He'd thought he'd use the skills when he and Jackie started up their business. Ignoring the bitter irony, he set to work.

Wayne interrupted an hour later to inform him the guest had cancelled.

"Did you find out anything?"

Roman nodded. "Dr. Reynolds has an office in San Francisco and one in San Diego. He has his own plane too."

Wayne grunted. "So he's a fat cat?"

"Yeah, but it looks like he earned his status. No marks on his record that I can find."

"Then why do you look like the cat that swallowed the cream?"

Roman let out a breath. "He hired a company to do some security work, an outfit called Security Plus. He was kind enough to give them a ringing endorsement, which they posted online. The guy who managed the company has an interesting name. Byron Lloyd."

THIRTEEN

That afternoon, Jackie was annoyed to find Mick hadn't yet returned to the lodge before she arrived in the kitchen. She wanted to pump him for more information on Asia. The campers were still packing up in her cabin, leaving her without a quiet place to do any further computer research. With no way to make progress on the investigation, she set to work helping June clean up after Skip had announced the snow-sculpture winner and the crowd began to disperse.

Skip said a quick hello on his way through the dining hall. "Competition went well, in spite of everything. Cross-country skiing is next. We're stop number two on the route." He checked his watch. "With the blizzard delay, I expect we've got a few hours until they arrive. June, where's Fallon? I need her help."

June looked up from slicing onions. "I don't know and I don't have time to go look for her."

"I will." Grateful to have a job to do, Jackie took off the towel she'd been using around her waist as an apron. "I'll check in her room first."

June nodded and returned to her cooking.

Jackie made her way down the hall to Fallon's room. She stood outside the partially opened door. "Fallon? Are you in there?"

No answer. After a loud knock, she poked her head in. The

bed was unmade, Fallon's pajamas lying discarded on the floor. It was hard to say if her warm jacket was missing in the jumble of clothing scattered around. Maybe the girl had gone out for some cross-country herself. The day was crisp and clear and she'd been cooped up with a houseful of guests all night. It made sense that she would have craved some fresh air and solitude.

In spite of Roman's warnings to stay inside, Jackie bundled up and walked into the dazzling day. The sight took her breath away. The whole property looked as if it had been bathed in sparkling sugar. The vivid green of snow-capped trees and the gray, shadowed mountain shone against a palette of pure white.

She was overcome by the beauty. In spite of everything, God blessed her with an exquisite scene that only He could have made. It was the same magical feeling felt so many times in the years she'd returned to this rugged place. The only thing more perfect would be sharing it the way she and Roman had in the past. Picturing him made her head swim.

Dax was busily shoveling snow, clearing a path to the front door. His breath showed in little puffs as he worked, plaid shirt pulled taught across his barrel chest.

"Hi, Dax. Getting ready for the skiers?"

He nodded. "Usually one or two come way ahead of the pack. Skip wants it ready in case they gotta use the facilities or come in for grub."

"Need help?"

"Nah."

"You haven't seen Fallon around, have you?"

"Not since yesterday before the blizzard."

Jackie sighed and started to move away.

He stopped her. "Fallon okay?"

"I'm not sure. June sent me to find her, but I haven't had any luck so far. She's probably out skiing somewhere. Why do you ask?"

He leaned on the handle of the shovel, squinting against the glare. "Something funny that happened. Most likely it's nothing. I don't have kids so I probably think everything they do is funny."

"What happened?"

"Skip asked me to get the mail while I was in town. I brought it back but I had a bunch of stuff in my pack so Fallon took it for me. I saw her thumb through the stack and then she kinda had a fit."

"What kind of fit?"

He crinkled his forehead. "Just sort of straightened up like she'd gotten an electric shock or something. Dropped the whole stack. I went to help her pick them up, but she waved me away."

Jackie frowned. "Something in the mail upset her?"

"Seemed that way." He sighed. "I could be all wrong. I think she mighta been crying. You think maybe I should have stopped her or told Skip? I'm no good with kids."

Jackie squeezed his arm. "I'm sure she wouldn't have talked about it anyway. Thanks for telling me."

Dax turned back to his shoveling.

Jackie walked in a confused fog back toward her cabin. Something wasn't right with the Delucchis. Deep down she felt Fallon's reaction was not just typical teen angst. Wishing Roman was there to consult on the prickly Fallon situation, she poked her head briefly into Riverrun and found two women still busily packing up their gear in preparation for the next flight out. It wouldn't be long. Out the window she could see Roman's plane approaching.

She described Fallon and asked the women if they'd seen her.

Neither one had. The tingle of worry in Jackie's stomach began to grow. She was just exiting the cabin when she noticed Byron Lloyd standing in the window of his own cabin, talking on the phone, a serious expression on his normally jovial face.

He saw her looking at him and nodded, turning his back so she could not read his expression further. With a burst of determination she knocked on his door.

He answered. "Hello, Ms. Swann. I thought you were avoiding me and here you are, right on my doorstep. Won't you come in?"

She started to decline, then reconsidered. It wouldn't hurt to take a peek at Lloyd's belongings. Maybe it would give her some insight into the fake reporter's real identity.

He held the door and ushered her in. The place was neat, no evidence of the men who had bunked there the previous night. Lloyd's bed was made, no dishes sat on the counter or in the sink. The only sign that anyone was staying in the place was Lloyd's sleek laptop on the table and a small, packed duffel bag near the bed.

He grinned. "Your young Roman can be a hothead. Bit of a rough-and-tumble last night."

He's not my Roman, she wanted to say. Instead, determined to take control of the conversation for a change, she folded her arms and stared directly at him. "Mr. Lloyd, I looked up the magazine you said you'd written for and they had no record of you."

He blinked. "That right?"

"Yes, that's right. There is no Byron Lloyd working for *Adventure Road Magazine* and there never has been. Why is that?"

"I see." Lloyd turned away and walked to the chair, sitting heavily. "So you've been investigating me? Why?"

"Answer the question."

He looked at her for a long moment, no trace of his usual smile. "It's easy to explain, really."

"I'm listening."

"I write under a pen name."

Jackie started. A pen name. She felt ridiculous for not considering that. Could he be telling the truth? She felt her cheeks flush with heat. "What is it?"

"Did you tramp through the snow all the way to my cabin to ask me what my pen name is? I'm flattered, really." He glanced out the window. "Fallon seemed almost as interested in my career as you are."

"Fallon?" Jackie was brought back to her original mission. "Have you seen her recently?"

He shifted, crossing his arms over his big stomach. "As a matter of fact, yes. Early this morning she was here, knocking on my door, asking to have a few minutes on my computer."

"Why would she do that? There's a computer in the lodge she can use."

He pursed his lips. "Said her parents took away her personal computer a few months back. I gathered she wanted to conduct some private business. Stayed about fifteen minutes, then left. That's the last I've seen of her this morning."

Jackie considered. "What sites did she visit?"

He shrugged. "As I said, that's her private business. I didn't ask and she didn't volunteer the information."

Jackie took a deep breath. "Look, Mr. Lloyd. You've been asking questions and popping up in private conversations since you got here. I'm pretty sure after she left you checked the search history on your computer, just to satisfy your own curiosity, maybe?"

A flush appeared in his cheeks. "Such a thing to say. I should take offense."

"I'm getting worried about Fallon. No one has seen her for hours and Dax said she'd been really upset. If you know something about where she might be, I think you'd better come clean about it."

He let out a long sigh, which ruffled the edges of his droopy mustache. "She spent some time poking around looking for info

on a city in Arizona. Place called Avondale." The sun streaming through the window painted his face in harsh light. "Then
she booked a flight there."

Roman landed and prepared to load the next set of passengers for a return trip to the airport. His growling stomach sent
him to the kitchen in search of a snack and, he hoped, time to
tell Jackie what he'd discovered about Lloyd. The tricky part
was how Jackie would react to his snooping.

He could sit on the information and do nothing. But what if
Lloyd was the shooter, waiting for another chance? Roman's
gut tightened. Lloyd wouldn't get another opportunity to hurt
Jackie. Not if Roman could help it. He met Jackie outside the
lodge, noticing right away the look of worry on her face.

"Roman, I'm glad you're here. I think I found out something
about Fallon that's going to upset June."

He watched her nervously twist a strand of hair. "What is it?"

She was about to tell him when June popped her head out
of the kitchen window. "Come in here, you two. On the double."

Roman followed Jackie to the kitchen, wondering what she'd
discovered about Fallon. The kitchen was warm, smelling of fresh-
baked bread that set his mouth watering. June sliced off a piece
of a golden loaf and handed it to him, along with a cup of coffee.

"Thanks, Mrs. D."

She smiled and patted him on the back. "Enjoy, sweetie."

Jackie fiddled with her slice, cheeks pink and a worried
frown creasing her forehead. She glanced at Roman and gave
him a distracted nod before turning her attention back to June.
"I, I think I need to tell you something."

June began to grate a block of cheese. "Fire away."

"I'm not sure…I could be wrong."

June continued to shred the cheese into pale yellow strands.
"What is it, hon? I've got to get these quiches in the oven."

"I've been looking for Fallon. I happened to stop by Lloyd's cabin."

Roman gulped coffee and burned his tongue. What had she been doing there?

Jackie took a step closer. "He said Fallon asked to use his computer. She wanted to research something."

June stopped working on the cheese and turned to Jackie, grater suspended in the air. "I don't know why, when she's got a perfectly good computer in the office."

"Lloyd said she wanted privacy."

June turned away from the counter. An inexplicable tone in her voice brought Roman to his feet. "What would she need to look at privately?"

"She was researching flight information."

"Flights? She wanted to fly somewhere?" Her voice was tense, like a tightly pulled thread.

Jackie continued after a moment of hesitation. "Lloyd thinks she wanted to go to Arizona, to Avondale."

"Arizona?" June's voice sank to a whisper. Her face paled to cream-white. "Not Arizona. Not that."

It was only Roman's quick action that kept June from striking her head on the floor as she crumpled. He managed to catch her around the shoulders and ease her down, resting her upper body against his knees.

He shot a look at Jackie. "Call for help."

At first he thought she hadn't heard him.

Then, with a look of mingled horror and anguish, Jackie nodded and ran from the room.

FOURTEEN

For the second time that week, Roman paced the tile floor of the hospital, only now he watched Jackie from the corner of his eye. She sat with her arms wrapped around herself, eyes fixed on a spot on a magazine-strewn table. He decided to try again, wishing she'd give him an inkling of her feelings so he'd know what to say.

"Do you want to go outside for some fresh air? We could walk for a while."

She shook her head no. He sank down next to her, hand caressing her cold fingers, wishing he could do anything to take her pain away. "It's not your fault. Don't blame yourself for June's situation."

She tried to speak but nothing came out. Tears rolled down her face and Roman gathered her in his arms, stroking her hair and rubbing circles on her back. "It's okay. It's going to be okay."

Jackie leaned into him and cried. He desperately tried to think of something to say that would ease her grief, but nothing would come so he held her close and let her weep.

When her shuddering sobs slowed, she excused herself to go splash water on her face.

Roman had tried calling Skip several times since June's collapse, but he did not answer his phone. Dax volunteered to track him down, suggesting perhaps he'd gone out to check the ski route or had snowmobiled into town for a forgotten item.

Fallon had not been found either, though Lloyd had offered to help. The big man had spoken in booming tones. "I'll go look for her. Maybe she's visiting one of the other cabins or taking a walk."

He didn't like the thought of Lloyd wandering around the lodge without anyone to keep an eye on him, but there was nothing that could be done about that at the moment. "Don't go too far," Roman had advised. The last thing they needed was another lost person. At least both Skip and Fallon knew something about how to survive an Alaska winter. He did not feel so confident about Lloyd's cold-weather savvy.

He replayed June's collapse again. *Not Arizona,* she'd said. *Not that.* What was in Arizona that frightened the woman so badly? He'd never heard any of the Delucchis speak of the place. Jackie had looked just as confused as he felt, so he was pretty sure she didn't know the connection either. Did it have something to do with the photo he'd seen in Fallon's room? The one she was desperate to hide?

His phone rang. It was Wayne. "I got your message. Stay there with the family. I'll get Jimmy to cover your flights for the day. June going to be okay?"

Roman kept his voice low and walked farther down the hall. "Don't know. She didn't regain consciousness during the flight here. I just wish we could get hold of Skip." He told Wayne of June's strange reaction to Jackie's news.

"Avondale? Why does that city ring a bell with me?" He paused. "I can't bring it up right now, but it will come to me eventually."

Roman knew his friend would kick the memory around until it resurfaced. "I know it will."

Wayne's tone changed. "How's Jackie taking it?"

He eyed her, hunched on the waiting room chair. "Not great. She's completely shut down. I don't know what to say to her."

Wayne blew out a breath. "Just be there for all of them." He added after a moment, "And take care of yourself."

Roman pocketed the phone, wondering if Wayne's last comment related to the situation or his emotions about Jackie. He didn't have much more time to think about it, as Skip came around the corner at a run.

"What's happened?" His eyes were wild and he panted hard. "Dax told me June collapsed."

Roman gripped his upper arm. "Yes. We got her here as quickly as we could. Doctors are in with her now and we're waiting to hear."

"Tell me everything."

Roman led Skip to the spot where Jackie sat. The sight of him jerked her out of her reverie. She stood and embraced him.

"Oh, Skip. I'm so glad you're here."

He pulled her to arm's length. "June's been working too hard. I knew I should have hired someone to help out, but she insisted she could handle it."

Roman shot a look at Jackie. "She, er, reacted badly to some news."

Skip started. "What? What news? What exactly happened?"

Jackie took a breath. "I was looking for Fallon and I came across some information that indicated she'd looked into flights to Arizona."

Skip took a step back as if he'd been slapped. "How did you find that out?"

Jackie told him about Lloyd. "And I went into the kitchen to tell June." Tears filled her eyes. "She collapsed. I'm so sorry."

Skip turned away from them and walked to the window. "It's all falling apart," he whispered, barely loud enough for Roman to hear. "Everything we've worked for."

Jackie approached him hesitantly. "What can I do? Is there anything at all?"

He continued to stare out the window. "Only pray. That's the only thing I can think of."

Jackie nodded and laid a hand on Skip's shoulder. She looked uncertainly at Roman.

He joined her, laying his hands on Skip's other shoulder, and Jackie prayed for June's recovery. She'd just gotten to the *amen* when two doctors approached and led them back to the sitting area.

Roman introduced Skip to the doctors.

The taller of the two smiled kindly. "Your wife has had a small stroke, Mr. Delucchi. She's resting comfortably. We'll have to wait a bit to see how the medicines we've given her have worked and if there is any lasting damage from the episode."

"A...a stroke?" Skip's face turned ashen. "How does that kind of thing happen?"

The doctor explained the physiology before he added, "Was your wife under significant stress? Stress can trigger this kind of event."

Skip blinked several times. "Yes. Yes she was." He sighed deeply. "Can I see her? Please?"

"The nurses are with her now, but I'll take you to her in a moment." The doctor drew Skip apart from the group and continued to talk.

Roman saw the ghastly look on Jackie's face. She'd gone completely pale, her eyes glittering intensely.

Dax appeared and stepped close to Roman, clearing his throat.

"Didn't want to barge in," he whispered. "What's the word?"

Roman told him the diagnosis.

Dax nodded solemnly. "Bad. So what's to be done?"

"Can you handle the cross-country racers? I know Skip will want to make good on his Winterfest commitments. I'll call

Wayne and ask if he can arrange to get some ladies from church over to the lodge to handle the cooking and such. Keep an eye out for Fallon if you can, and call me if she appears. I'll make some calls from here and try to track her down."

"Right." Dax shifted and shoved his hands into his pockets. "What about the guests?"

"Wayne is sending Jimmy to fly them out."

"All except that Lloyd character."

Roman raised an eyebrow. "You don't think much of him?"

"Nosy. Always askin' questions."

"About whom?"

"Jackie, mostly. He wanted to know if she'd been to the lodge recently, did she stay anywhere else, that kind of thing."

Roman fought a rising anger. "Did you tell him anything?"

Dax gave him a crooked smile. "What?" He tapped his ear with a finger. "I can't hear so good. Old war injury."

Roman laughed. "Good man. Call me if anything comes up."

Dax sighed. He walked to Skip, clasped him tightly on the arm and then left, as a nurse came to escort Skip in to see his wife.

Roman turned around to check on Jackie, but she was gone.

She didn't know how she'd gotten there, but Jackie found herself in a tiny chapel, soft light shining on the gleaming wood altar. The room was empty and silent. Her legs shook so badly she hardly made it to the front before they gave out, and she sank on her knees to the carpeted floor.

"Oh, God," she prayed. "Help us. Help us, please." She was unable to finish the prayer as tears choked off the words. She rocked slowly back and forth, feeling terrible fear and guilt. She knew her information had caused June's stroke. The weight of it pressed her down. When she thought the sensation would completely overwhelm her, she felt a strong hand on her back.

She looked up to find Roman, worry written across his face, as he knelt beside her.

"Jackie, June is going to be okay. The doctors are hopeful that she'll recover. Skip is with her now."

"But…it's all my fault." She couldn't finish. The tears flowed in hot trails down her cheeks.

Roman slowly wrapped her in a tight embrace. "No, honey. It was not your fault. You told June about Fallon because it was the right thing to do. There was no other choice."

"I should have waited, tried to find Skip." Shuddering sobs shook her frame. "What will happen now? To the Delucchis and Fallon? I feel so guilty."

He laid his cheek against her forehead. "They'll get through this. Don't worry. You're not thinking clearly. It's the shock."

She pressed her face against his chest, listening to the steady beat of his heart. His presence pushed the darkness back. She had the oddest notion that as long as she could stay there, close to him, things really would be okay. His gentle caress eased the words out of her before she could think about them. "Roman, I feel lost, like I did when Danny died."

He stiffened and let go of her. Climbing to his feet he offered a hand to help her up. The light shone in his eyes as he took hold of her arms and turned her to face him.

"That's why I don't want you to take all this on yourself, Jackie. Guilt is a terrible burden. It makes you feel like you're cut off from everything you love. When Danny died I couldn't feel anything but guilt that was so bad it seemed like I had a knife through my heart. I'd wake up praying that it wasn't true, that I hadn't killed your brother."

The anguish on his face took her breath away. "Roman, I'm so sorry."

She looked at the altar, bathed in golden light, and then at Roman, who stared at it hungrily as if he desperately wanted to

reach out and warm himself by its glow. His pain had been un-
bearable, and she'd been too focused on her own sorrow to care.

The thought stirred inside her. "God will forgive, Roman."

He was silent for so long she wondered if he'd heard her.

"Yes," he said in a voice so low it was no more than a whisper.
"They say God forgives." He turned away. "But people don't."

Though the words bit hard at her soul, she knew he was right.
As much as she drew comfort from him, and felt embers of the
love that they'd shared, she had not forgiven him, any more than
her father had.

As she watched his slumped shoulders as he headed for the
door, she realized that he hadn't forgiven himself, either.

FIFTEEN

June was still unconscious when Roman and Jackie left the hospital at Skip's insistence. Roman had to agree that their presence was accomplishing nothing. After their encounter in the chapel, Roman felt drained, vulnerable, as if some bricks had fallen from the wall he'd built around himself. The last thing he wanted to do was bare his soul to Jackie, the woman who had more reason than anyone to hate him. Deep down he knew that the only way to draw closer to her again would be to unearth all the pain and anguish and hold it up to the light. The question was, was he strong enough to do it? He avoided looking at her. There was work to be done.

They hustled back to the plane and were in the air shortly. Already the sky was darkening into a dusk that seemed endless.

"Where could Fallon be?" Jackie said, peering into the wind driven snow below.

He sighed. "I've called a few places in town. They haven't seen her."

"Could she have made it to the airport?"

He considered. "I don't see how. Too far to snowmobile, and I checked with all the pilots who've been shuttling guests so she didn't get out that way."

Jackie shook her head. "Why would she want to run, anyway? And what's in Arizona that she's so desperate to see?"

He thought about the photo she'd quickly hidden from him. "A friend she met online?" The explanation didn't seem feasible. "Call Dax and see if he's heard anything, will you?"

Jackie phoned him. She covered the mouthpiece. "He says there's no sign of her. He's got everything under control with the skiers and a few people have arrived to help with cooking. So they're okay for the moment, but he'll need help getting the cabins ready later."

"Ask him what Lloyd's up to."

She started, then relayed the message, listening carefully before hanging up. "He hasn't seen him since we flew out this morning. He didn't show up for lunch. Do you know something about Lloyd?"

Way to go, Roman. Dig yourself in deep again. "I wondered about him, is all. Why he's so interested in you and Fallon. I looked into it."

Jackie's eyes widened and a pink flush crept into her cheeks. "What? Tell me what you found out?"

"Lloyd used to run a security company. Worked for your boss once upon a time."

The life seemed to leak out of Jackie. She slumped against the seat and closed her eyes. "I knew it. All that garbage about a pen name. I knew he was lying." Her eyes snapped open and she turned on him. "Why didn't you tell me about your snooping?"

"I wasn't snooping. I was trying to protect Fallon…. You dropped this situation on my lap, remember?"

She folded her arms across her chest. "You should have told me what you were up to. What if Lloyd found out you were investigating him? Mick says we have to be careful."

He grunted. "You can continue to scheme with Mick and see if he can get you out of the mess you've gotten yourself into, but he's only going to make things worse."

"You don't trust him, do you?"

"No, and maybe you shouldn't either. I don't see him or your friend Asia doing anything to help out."

"They're trying to protect me."

"Then why hasn't Asia shown up here to get you out of trouble? She's the one who started this mess."

She opened her mouth to retort, then closed it abruptly.

They remained in stony silence for the rest of the flight. He wanted to shake her. Stubborn, independent, foolish woman. "Look. I know they're your friends. I just don't want to see you get hurt."

There was no point in attempting to reason with her, so he settled on trying to figure out where he could search next for the missing Fallon. He was relieved when they touched down on the landing strip and found a Range Rover waiting. Without a word between them, they climbed aboard and headed back to the lodge.

Several pink-cheeked skiers poled their way past the vehicle, their reflective gear catching the light from the newly risen moon. Roman nodded to them, feeling grateful that at least Dax had been able to keep the cross-country race going. When he stopped, Jackie unstrapped her seat belt, her shoulders stiff with anger. He'd gone around to open the door for her when her phone rang.

The look on her face almost made him smile. Clearly she didn't want to answer it in front of him, but her fear of missing the call must have outweighed her annoyance. After shooting him a look, she answered.

Though Roman took a step away to give her a modicum of privacy, she knew he could hear every word of her conversation. She stuck out her chin and gestured him closer, holding the phone between them. "Mick? Roman is here with me." She related the morning's events.

"So Roman's listening in, huh? What is up with the people

in this town? Never a moment's privacy. I had to practically fend that girl off with a ski pole."

Jackie straightened. "What girl?"

"The one from the lodge. The Delucchis' kid."

She exchanged a look with Roman. "When did you see her?"

"At the crack of dawn this morning. She knocked on my door, asking if she could stay here and get a ride into town. Can you believe it? I don't even know her."

"You turned her away?"

"Of course I did. I can't have a teen girl staying with me."

"Where did she go?"

"Not sure. She was on snowshoes, so not far, I'm guessing."

Jackie checked her watch. It was a little after one. "I've got to go. Fallon's missing. Call me if she shows up there again."

"Wait, Jackie. I need to talk to you."

Jackie eyed Roman, who was staring at her. "I'll call you soon. Promise." She hung up on his protests.

Roman raised an eyebrow. "Not very neighborly of him to kick Fallon out."

"Never mind that. We've got to find her."

His brow furrowed as he surveyed the horizon. "The hunting cabin is too far for her to snowshoe into town. There's nothing else between here and there except miles of snow and…" His eyes closed for a moment as if he'd experienced a sharp pain.

It came to her at the same moment. "The cabin."

The unfinished cabin that had remained fixed in time, just as it had been the day Roman and her brother had left there and slid off the road. Her mouth felt filled with cotton. "You don't suppose…she went there?"

His voice sounded hollow and oddly emotionless as he stared into the distance. "It would make sense, some shelter until she could get someone to take her to the airport. Maybe waiting until my plane returned."

"No phone there?"

"No. It was never finished. Skip said they ran out of money but I think he couldn't bear to work on it after… everything."

Unfinished, like Danny's life. Waiting for closure. The idea took her by surprise. She thought she'd had closure—Danny was dead, Roman was to blame, end of story. Could there be another chapter in their lives together? One that didn't end with bitterness? A snowflake floated down and landed on her cheek, freeing her from her reverie. "We've got to go see."

Roman's voice was still flat. "I'll go."

"Me too."

He shook his head, still not meeting her eyes. "It's dangerous. Snow hasn't been cleared regularly. There's a convex slope up there, and we've had a lean snow winter. Prime conditions for an avalanche. Stay here. I'm going to get some gear from the lodge, and then I'll go."

Anger churned inside her again. He would not tell her what to do, especially not now, in the place that had taken her brother. She would not let him have control over her future ever again. "I'll get some snowshoes and then I'm going, no matter what you think about it."

Her pride refused to let her stand there like a child waiting for a ride after school. With an uneasy feeling, she made her way to the cabin. The women had cleared out and left the place empty and quiet. Her skin prickled as she stepped inside, wondering if someone had picked the new lock as easily as they had done before. She hurriedly put water and some protein bars into a pack, grabbed her snowshoes and bundled up. Jackie yearned to call Mick and find out what Asia had told him, but she didn't dare get caught up in a conversation. Roman would likely leave without her.

She pushed herself to move, quickly checking her messages on her satellite phone to see if there was any news there as she let herself out of the cabin and locked the door. One from Skip saying he'd stay at the hospital for a few more hours and then join in the search for Fallon. His voice was hoarse and strained. She felt the surge of responsibility again as she remembered June sliding to the kitchen floor. There was one more message. *Don't tell anyone about the thumb drive. If you want to live.* She forced herself to breathe, scanning the tree line, remembering the shot that almost took her life.

It could have been either a male or female voice, a low whisper that seemed to echo in her mind.

If you want to live.

The message brought it all back. She was one step away from someone who wanted her silent.

Reynolds's hired guns were getting closer. It was possible they'd been responsible for shooting her. The wide expanse of snow-covered ridgeline provided a bounty of places to hide and to ready a rifle. Lloyd hadn't been seen all morning. He could be out there right now, poised to fire the shot that would kill her. A chill raced up her spine and set the hair on her neck on end. She wanted more than anything to run back into the cabin and pull the curtains closed. But what about Fallon? Danny had cared for Fallon. There was no way she could abandon the girl, and Skip was probably half crazy with worry.

Was Roman right? Had her secrecy and faith in her friends brought danger to the people at Delucchi's? She heard the rumble of a snowmobile engine. If she didn't hurry, Roman would leave without her. Maybe it was better for him to go alone, to take care of Fallon without the added danger of her presence.

Her mind swam.

Roman shouldn't go alone.

If he was buried in snow, she would be his only chance of

rescue. Backcountry rules were clear. Never travel alone in avalanche territory.

Her feet felt frozen to the ground.

Lord, what do I do?

The feeling that came over her was strong, though it did not erase the fear that slithered inside her like a poisonous snake.

She hurried toward the snowmobiles, where Roman waited.

SIXTEEN

Roman experienced a sense of detachment as they raced upslope toward the unfinished cabin. He had returned a half dozen times since the accident, trying to reconstruct from bits of memory the events of that night. Each time it was the same, a deep misery that invaded his mind and body. On this trip, with Jackie yards behind him, he felt numb. It was an effort to force his mind to focus on the surroundings, the wind, slope and piles of snow that could release their pressure unexpectedly with the force of an atom bomb. Using a flashlight, he checked a crystal of snow that landed on his dark jacket sleeve. Instead of the welcome star-shaped flake, these were small. Small and dangerous, the kind that could cling together in a tight shelf of snow that might break free from its loose underlayer with deadly consequences.

About a half mile from the cabin, he pulled the snowmobile under the shelter of a massive pine. "Can't take the road, it hasn't been cleared in a couple years." He swallowed hard. "We've got to go on foot from here—too dangerous to risk vibrating the snow with the engines." He got out two bright red avalanche cords and tied one to his own belt, handing the other one to Jackie, along with the pack. "I didn't have time to get the beacons. These will have to do. If one of us is buried, hopefully the red cord will show on the surface long enough to attempt a rescue. There are bare-bones safety supplies in the pack. Keep it with you." He hoped the shock value of the cords would change her mind as he looped hers around her small waist, the feel of her in the circle of his arms making his pulse pound.

If she was afraid, she didn't show it. She kept her chin up as he fastened on the rope, a defiant glint in her eyes.

They headed up the steep slope toward the cabin, which stood silent and snow-covered in a glade of trees.

"Why did Skip pick this spot to build a cabin?"

"The view." He gestured to the undisturbed sweep of pristine snow and trees, backed by the rugged, moonlit mountain.

"But doesn't the slope make it dangerous in avalanche country?"

"He intended to cut another road along the top of the ridge, put up a snow fence—that kind of thing. When we came up in winter to work on it, we'd make sure to clear the snow before-hand with explosives." He had a picture of Danny, his face lit like a kid on Christmas morning watching Skip detonate the charges. The pain cut a raw path inside him as he recalled the exuberant teen Danny had been.

She must have read his mind. "Yeah," she said softly. "I remember my brother loved that. Any opportunity to blow things up was just fine with him." She cleared her throat. "Did you help build the Delucchi Lodge?"

Roman shook his head. "Only the cabin. Helped get supplies and things, but they had some people working for them. A lady housekeeper whom I only met once and a couple guys. Don't think they live here anymore."

Jackie mercifully stopped asking questions as they trekked single file toward the cabin. When they drew close enough that only a wide, snow-covered slope separated them from their destination, Roman stopped and tried again.

"You stay here. The more people that cross this snow, the more unstable it becomes. I'll go check it out and come back."

Her eyes narrowed. "I'm coming too."

His hands balled into fists. "Why…?" He wanted to say, *Why are you doing this to me? Why are you forcing me to be with you, responsible for your safety here? Right here? Where I failed all of you?*

He kept his voice level. "She may not even be in the cabin. Why risk it?"

"You said it yourself. It's avalanche country. No one should travel alone."

He eyed the sheet of white in front of them and poked the end of his snowshoe into the white powder. It slid in readily, which meant a loose layer lurked underneath the compacted crust. Sugar snow, a north-facing slope and plenty of accumulation, thanks to the blizzard. It all added up to a disaster in the making. Would it be the second tragedy to occur in this terrible spot? He could see it in his mind so clearly.

"Can you fly me to town?" Danny had said, showing up unexpectedly at the cabin where Roman was putting up Sheetrock for Skip.

"Why?"

"Need to do a favor for a friend."

They'd gotten into the truck and begun their descent down the road, which had been recently cleared of snow. The sun would set soon; Roman drove carefully, rounding the blind turn with care.

Then it happened. Something, some object in the road caused him to slam on his brakes. Then they were sliding, rolling and pitching into darkness.

Jackie's hand on his arm made him jerk to the present. Her eyes seemed to penetrate right through him. "Are you remembering that night?" she asked softly.

He cleared his throat. "Must be the location. How are you doing being up here?"

She thought for a moment. "Sad, but mostly I still feel angry."

He looked away from her face, wishing for the millionth time that he was not responsible for her pain. He deserved that anger and he would bear it. Ask the Lord for forgiveness, Wayne had advised many a time. But he would not ask, because he did not deserve it, any more than he deserved Jackie's absolution for what he'd done. It was finished, like snow after it had fallen.

Focus, Roman. You've got to keep your mind sharp to get through this.

He gave it one more shot. "I'm going to cross. It would be better for you to stay here, with the phone. Call if anything happens." When she opened her mouth to protest, he added, "If you're stubborn enough to come, at least wait until I've crossed. And remember, if we do have an avalanche, try to get to the trees and cover your nose and mouth."

"I remember. I took the wilderness survival class too."

He eyed the deceptively peaceful scene. The smallest trigger could set off a chain reaction if the conditions were right, and no amount of preparation or training could prevent that.

He turned his back and, with foreboding strong in his gut, he set out across the snow.

Jackie felt her stomach tense as she watched Roman head across the slope, his feet moving in a slow and steady rhythm. The impossibility of the situation caught up with her. A week ago she was working in a San Francisco office. Now here she was, hiding from someone who wanted her dead, listening for the rumble of an avalanche in a frozen Alaska nowhere.

With Roman.

She'd worked so hard to put it all behind her, the accident

and, most of all, her love for him. And she'd succeeded at funneling her feelings into anger—a bright, intense rage that lit her from the inside. But why was she here? And why was her heart thudding madly as she watched Roman's tall form press through the frozen night?

Many times, in the darkest of moments, she wondered what would have happened if Roman had been the one killed in the wreck and her brother the survivor. The idea did not bring her comfort. Danny was gone and Roman too, as far away now as he could possibly be. She imagined a wall of snow sweeping down to carry him away and a feeling stirred inside her. What was it? Fear? Longing? Love? In spite of the crushing grief, she'd desperately wanted to hear from Roman in the two long years following Danny's death. Along with the pain and anger, a trace of her love for Roman remained in the part of her that called out to him.

A small puff of snow broke free and slid several yards. Her whole body tensed as Roman stopped, watching. When it was clear no more was coming, he continued on his way.

Jackie tried to still the wild thumping in her chest. *Focus on Fallon. We've got to find her and get her out of here.*

And they'd have to tell her about her mother, she reminded herself. The knowledge sat in her stomach like a cold stone. How would Fallon react to the news? And why had she embarked on this ridiculous notion to run away in the first place?

Roman reached the far side and waved at Jackie to follow. She stepped out into the snow and kept her pace slow and steady to keep the fear at bay. *Just keep your eyes on Roman.*

He stood, gaze riveted on her, at the far side, body tense and hands partially outstretched, as if he could pluck her out of danger if the slope gave way. Closer and closer she walked, until she could see the lines etched in his forehead, the shock of dark hair that lay across his face.

Finally, after an eternity, she'd made it across. He took her hand and helped her to the shelter of the trees. He didn't speak, but the relief in his face was palpable.

They made quick progress up to the cabin, arriving in minutes at the door. Roman knocked. "Fallon? Are you in there?"

There was no answer.

He knocked again, louder.

Nothing.

Jackie groaned. "All that effort and she's not here? Where could she be? Lost in the snow somewhere?"

They stepped off the porch and were about to head toward the treacherous crossing when Roman caught her arm.

"Look."

She would have missed it completely. Stamped on the snow was the imprint of a snowshoe.

Roman looked grim. "She's in there, all right. We've got to go look."

He stepped back up on the porch and knocked one more time. "Fallon, I know you're in there. Jackie's with me and we've got to talk to you. We're coming in." He turned the handle and Jackie followed him into the cabin.

The place was cold, bare walls cutting the wind but not enough to insulate against the frigid temperatures. Sheets of plywood covered the windows and kept out the light, bathing the small family room in shadow. Roman pointed to a hallway that led to the back. They walked quietly, though Jackie was not sure why. Fallon was not in the tiny bedroom. Jackie peeked into the bathroom and found it empty as well. They doubled back to check the kitchen.

Roman picked up an empty water bottle. "Well, someone's been home."

A packet of peanuts and two apples lay on the table. "So where is she?"

He went to the pantry closet and opened the door, listening for a moment, before he sat down in a chair. "Fallon, we're here and we're staying. We can eat peanuts and apples and hang out all night until your dad can take over. Either way, it's going to get pretty cold up there."

The silence extended so long Jackie was about to speak, but Roman held a finger to his lips.

A creaking of wood and a sudden gust of freezing air floated out of the closet and Fallon climbed down the ladder. When she turned to face them, her nose was red from the cold and her eyes were swollen as if she'd been crying.

She planted her hands on her hips and glared at them. "What are you doing here?"

Jackie would have laughed if the girl hadn't looked so dead serious. "We could ask you the same question. Your parents have been looking all over for you."

She sniffed. "Oh, really? They needed someone to peel potatoes, I guess?"

Jackie fought the urge to shake the girl by the shoulders. She kept her tone light. "No, they've been worried about you, like all of us. We would never have guessed you'd be here, except that Mick told us you'd gone to him and we figured out the rest."

"I thought he was a cool guy. He was Mr. Friendly at the Winterfest. When I show up to ask him a favor, he practically slams the door in my face. What a loser."

Roman raised an eyebrow. "I think you surprised him."

"No kidding."

Jackie took a breath. "How did you think he was going to be able to help you?"

"I just needed a ride. He's got the snowmobile—it wouldn't kill him to run me to town. I would have taken one from the lodge, but Dax and Lloyd were out on them."

Lloyd knew how to ride a snowmobile? She wondered where

he'd gone in the wee hours of the morning when Fallon had snuck out. She put away the thought to revisit later. "Why were you headed to town?"

She shrugged.

Roman shook his head. "I could have flown you."

"I didn't want my parents to know, and you would go right over and tell them."

He nodded. "Yes, I would. They're your parents and they have a right to know what you're up to."

Fallon's lip trembled. "I knew you'd say that."

Jackie tried a gentler tone. "We need to talk to you about your mother."

"I don't want to hear it."

Roman held up a calming hand. "Let's not waste time. Point is, you've been busily making plans to run away, everyone has been going crazy trying to find you and you owe your parents some sort of explanation. Your mother…"

Fallon cut him off, her feet wide apart, eyes flashing. "I don't owe them anything, do you hear me? Not anything."

Jackie recoiled a step from the anger in Fallon's tone. "I'm pretty sure every teenager hates their parents at one time or another. Plenty have considered running away, too. Whatever is bothering you, you can work it out with your folks, but we need to…"

Tears began to run down Fallon's face. "No, no, no. They've lied to me my whole life. It's because of them that this all happened." She gestured wildly to the cabin.

"What?" Roman said, frowning. "What do you mean?"

"It's their fault that I had to ask him. I couldn't figure out how to do it myself." She cried, anguished sobs that seemed to be wrenched out of her. "If only I hadn't asked him. He'd be alive."

Jackie fought through her confusion. "Asked who?"

Fallon closed her eyes and hugged herself. "Danny."

SEVENTEEN

Roman shot a look at Jackie that was no doubt as confused as her own. What was the girl talking about? They would not be getting any sense out of her now, as she had become hysterical, crying so hard she got the hiccups. She was as close as he'd ever get to having a sister, and as much as he wanted to pepper her with questions, he felt the urge rise inside to comfort her. He took her hand and gave it a squeeze. "It's going to be okay."

Fallon squeezed back as if she was hanging on the edge of a cliff. Jackie dug a package of tissues out of her pocket and handed some to Fallon before she stroked the girl's shoulders.

Roman checked his watch and tried to keep his tone gentle. "Listen, I know you're upset and it seems like your problems are too big to tackle. I'll help you to figure out whatever needs to be done, I promise. Can you trust me now, Fallon?"

She blinked several times and nodded.

"Okay. Right now we've got to get moving." *And before the slope gets any more unstable.*

Fallon shook her head. "I'm not going back."

Jackie raised an eyebrow at Roman and he nodded slightly and cleared his throat. "Honey, your mom's taken sick. She's at the hospital and we'll need to take you to see her."

Fallon's head shot up. "Sick? What do you mean sick?"

Jackie exhaled. "She's had a problem with her heart. The doctors think she's going to be okay, but they needed her to stay for a while. Your father's there with her, but he sent us to find you."

Fallon's face went white. "Like a heart attack?"

"A small stroke," Jackie explained. "She'll be okay."

"How…how did it happen?" Fallon's voice was a whisper.

Roman stood. "We'll tell you all the details and everything after we get back to the lodge."

Jackie nodded. "Right now, we've got to get across that snowbank as quickly as we can."

They helped Fallon retrieve her backpack and strap on her snowshoes, and he repeated his safety instructions for her and attached an avalanche cord to her waist.

"Fallon, you go first. Head in a straight line as high up on the slope as you can. Wait for us by the snowmobiles once you get across. Can you do that?"

She nodded, dazed.

Jackie stood next to Roman as they watched her cross. The full moon had emerged from behind the clouds and lit the whole area in luminous white and silver. "That was really sweet, the way you handled Fallon."

He shrugged, risking a quick glance at her. "She's hurting about something. I hate to see her like that." Jackie's face was tilted to one side, the moon bringing out a glow in her hair, flooding his senses with a wave of longing.

"And you really will try to help her sort it all out, won't you?"

"I'll do my best." He heard her sigh, the tiniest sound, which was snatched away quickly by the cold wind. Then it was Jackie's turn to cross and she moved away, growing ever smaller against the white expanse that threatened to swallow her up.

He exhaled in relief when she'd reached safety. No matter what happened now, the two women could get back to the lodge on their own. Leaving the shadow of the unfinished cabin behind, he stepped out in the snow.

Jackie zipped her jacket tighter as she watched Roman begin his trek. In the eerie light, his shadow was long and dark, like a trail of smoke against the white. How odd, how very odd to see him here, in the Alaska wild that had been home to them both, in the exact spot where their future had died along with her brother. She was surprised when a tear trickled down her face. She turned her back to Fallon and wiped it away. It was not the time to sink into an emotional morass. There were far too many problems to deal with now.

Keep your eyes fixed on Roman.

Avalanche safety required that a person watch and track the exact position of her partner. Careful attention to location could mean the difference between life and death. Eyes stinging from the cold and the moisture collected on her lashes, she saw him stepping methodically, with the practiced gait of an experienced snowshoer. He was only a few yards from their spot under the trees. The furrowing of his brows gave him the look of a worried schoolboy. In spite of herself, she smiled.

A sudden vicious gust of wind knocked a shelf of snow loose. The sound took a moment to penetrate her senses. The snow gave way with a sharp crack that escalated until it became a roar, filling every inch of the space around them. Frozen in terror, she watched a section of snow break away and careen down the hillside in a steadily increasing mass. Roman turned his anguished face to her and shouted.

"Get behind a tree and hold on, both of you."

Somehow, she dragged Fallon to her feet and tried to get her to a more sheltered spot. There was no time. They were slammed against a pine, the force of the cascade pinning them there, forcing the breath out of their lungs. All they could do was try to brace against the massive blow that pushed against them with the strength of a runaway locomotive. Jackie tried desperately to keep Roman in her sight, but he was obliterated by the mass of white and swept from her view.

She struggled to keep her hands by her face, to maintain a pocket of air in case they were buried. Visions of an avalanche she'd witnessed as a child filled her mind. One moment, two skiers had been making their way across a perfect, untouched slope. The next they were gone, carried away by a rush of snow that engulfed them as if they'd never existed. One had been found dead hours later. The other, disappeared until the spring thaw revealed his body.

She tried to shield Fallon as snow continued to thunder past them, whipping against her face in an angry rush. The sound was deafening, and cold seemed to imbed itself in her body, sharp pieces of ice pricking her face and hands.

She thought she heard Fallon cry out, but it might have been the shriek of the fearful inundation.

Just as she thought she could withstand the terrible bombardment no longer, the sound tapered away, slower and slower until the thundering vibrations ceased. A profound quiet stole over them. It took a moment for her to realize she was still alive. Fallon was scrunched in her arms and they were pushed against a tree so tightly the girl's cheek was pressed into the bark. Snow encased them in all directions, but mercifully had not piled higher than her neck.

"Fallon," she gasped, after spitting out a mouthful of snow. "Are you okay?"

Jackie heard no reply. She wiggled a hand down and reached Fallon's hair. "Talk to me. Are you hurt?"

Fallon managed a mumble. "What happened?"

"Avalanche. We've got to get out of here." Jackie began thrashing back and forth to loosen the snow that held them prisoner. The weight of a thousand pounds of snow fought against her. Fortunately, the sturdy pine trunk had provided an obstruction that had diverted much of the flow around and farther down the slope. Clawing and batting like cornered animals, Fallon and Jackie slashed their way out, using the tree as a ladder. They emerged, panting, at the top of the pile.

Jackie sucked in a grateful breath. Fallon appeared to be in one piece, except for a cut on her face and a rapidly swelling lip. The relief turned immediately into fear as she surveyed the landscape, which suddenly seemed completely unfamiliar.

"Roman?" she yelled as loudly as she could. She strained to hear against the soft shush of snow that continued to trickle down past them. "Roman?" Her voice rang out, high and tinged with panic, echoing back at her.

They hurried back upslope as best they could to survey the slide area. Jackie worried at any moment the snow might come to life again in another avalanche.

Fallon was the first to speak. "I, I don't see him."

The area was a wall of white, no longer smooth and serene, but uneven, with piles of hardpack snow that had broken away before the slide. Jackie pulled a flashlight out of her pack and began scanning the snow. "Keep looking."

The tension in her stomach was now wire-tight. Everywhere she looked was nothing but an endless stretch of silvered snow, still slowly shifting and settling. She called Roman's name with increasing ferocity. "He's got to be here. Look for the cord."

Fallon climbed into the lower branches of the nearest tree, looking in all directions.

Jackie bit back a scream. "Can you see him?"

The girl remained silent for a long moment before she slid down. "There's nothing but snow."

No, no, no, her mind screamed. He could not be gone in that merciless rush. She ran to the next uneven hump of snow and strained every muscle to catch sight of him. A series of unwelcome facts flooded her mind.

Only a very small portion of buried avalanche victims survive, and the chance of survival drops with every passing minute. Suffocation, hypothermia, internal injuries, all the ugly terms her wilderness survival instructor hammered home stabbed at her. The seconds ticked away in time to the wild beating of her heart.

If she could just catch the tiniest glimpse, the smallest hint about where he lay buried, she could save him. Her eyes began to burn and tear. Again she moved to a different position and stared in every direction the flow might have taken him. She spotted one of their snowmobiles, overturned and wedged against a split tree. It had been carried along on top of the avalanche. If it still worked, it would get Fallon out safely.

Jackie knew she herself would not go. She could not ride away and leave Roman here, entombed in this angry place. A rage filled her up and spilled out into a shriek. "You took my brother," she shouted at the mountain. "You won't take Roman too."

In spite of the threat of a new slide, she raced to a pine tree and heaved herself up onto the lowest branch that would support her weight.

Fallon watched, openmouthed.

Jackie stabbed a finger toward the snowmobile. "Go see if it works," she commanded, before she continued up as high as she dared. All around banks of snow filled her vision, broken only by the deep shadow of the trees. The minutes groaned by in painful slow motion. She tried to reconstruct where he'd been when the flow started, but the terrain looked vastly different. Would she even be able to see the avalanche cord in the moonlight?

Tears pricked her eyes. He was out there, dying, and she could not find the smallest sign of him in the deadly whiteness. "Roman?" she screamed again, though she knew he could not answer. "Where are you?" The only answer was the soft whoosh of the rising wind, toying with the newly fallen snow.

In a far corner of her mind she heard an engine fire to life.

"It works," Fallon yelled over the noise.

Despair began to fill her up. *Roman, Roman.* She should have been able to feel his spirit, the buoyant, steadfast heart that had seemed to beat only for her in the past. Instead she felt nothing, no whisper, no shadow of where he lay buried in the snow. Her breath grew short, she felt dizzy.

"Jackie?" Fallon's voice was small and childlike as she looked up at Jackie from the base of the tree.

Startled out of her reverie, Jackie was about to order Fallon back to the lodge when she saw it.

A tiny whisper of red, dark against the snow like a spot of blood on a pure white cloth.

Her breath froze. "I see the cord. I see it." She shimmied down the tree, heedless of the rough bark cutting through her jacket, and ran, half falling, toward the red spot, praying the moon would stay clear of the clouds for a few more moments. After several yards she whirled around, eyes aching, unable to find the mark. There was only a blur of white everywhere she looked. Fighting panic, she ran back to the tree, and Fallon climbed with her.

Please let me find it. Please, Lord, let me find it.

The small string of color shone on the snow.

"There," she nearly shrieked. "There it is! See it? Stay up here and guide me."

Fallon remained in the tree while Jackie raced down again and dropped into the snow.

"Left, more left," Fallon called.

Jackie took step after step, following Fallon's directions until she spotted it again. Walking as fast as she could, trying not to unsettle the snow any further, she arrived at the gleam of the red avalanche cord. She dropped to her knees, ripped open the pack Roman had given her and put together the small shovel. When Fallon reached the spot, she used her hands to dig while Jackie shoveled furiously.

Soon several feet of the red cord was revealed. Snow flying, fingers numb, Jackie worked until the sweat ran down her face.

Puffs of white came from Fallon's mouth and her cheeks reddened with the effort. She dug with frantic animal motions, burrowing further and further into the snow.

They continued down several feet and Jackie knew they were close. A form began to materialize like an eerie three-dimensional snow angel. Fallon stopped. Her voice dropped to a whisper. "Jackie."

"Keep digging. We're almost there."

"Jackie," Fallon said more urgently.

Jackie stopped shoveling long enough to look at Fallon.

Her face was deadly pale, mouth open in a horrified O. "What if he's…?"

What if? The words finally penetrated her racing thoughts. Should a girl, a child really, have to face the possible answer to that tortured question? She stopped the horror before it could trickle through her body and hesitated only a moment before she made the decision. "It's going to be okay. Take the snowmobile back to the lodge and get Dax. Come and get us."

Fallon didn't move. Her glance shifted from Jackie to the snow-covered form. "I'm not sure…"

"Go now," Jackie commanded. "Hurry."

Fallon stood and ran toward the trees. Jackie resumed her digging but Fallon's question rang in her mind.

What if?

EIGHTEEN

Roman had only enough time to shout a warning to Jackie before the wall of snow crashed into him. Then he was engulfed in a frigid tide, swept along as if he was part of the mountain itself.

Soon the violent motion disoriented him and he had only a vague impression of pain as he struck rocks and fallen logs in his frantic slide, twisting and turning as he went until all sense of direction was lost. It seemed to go on endlessly before he slammed to a halt and a crushing weight settled down on him.

Though he'd managed to keep his arms up, the air pocket around his head was small, any moonlight blotted out by the mass of material that imprisoned him. He could not move, not even shift his arm to try to break free. The weight was too much.

His brain put the dire facts together. He estimated he would be alive for approximately eighteen more minutes until he died of suffocation from breathing in his own exhaled carbon dioxide. Or perhaps his warm breath would melt the surrounding snow first, until it refroze into a cocoon of ice that would seal out the air. The layers of snow would muffle any sounds he might make. He was entombed as effectively as if he'd been dropped into a coffin and covered over with earth.

Oddly, Roman felt no panic about his imminent death. He realized he'd been waiting for punishment in one way or another since the night Danny died. It was somehow fitting that he would die on this mountaintop, just as his friend had done.

He closed his eyes and went back to that night. Danny, next to him in the truck. Rounding the corner. A vehicle racing up in the other direction, too fast, too close. Roman swerved, the tires skidding over the ice, sending them down the slope to the rocks below. A vague memory stirred in his dazed mind. A shadow where it shouldn't have been. A person's shadow. Watching. Watching them. Watching as Danny died. His vision grew fuzzy, as his own breath began to poison him.

The snow seemed to settle more tightly around him, pushing the breath from his lungs, hurrying his death along. He did not consider praying for rescue—he knew he was not worthy of God's mercy. Not anymore.

Roman closed his eyes. His thoughts turned to Jackie.

Had she gotten to cover? Had Fallon?

More snow sifted down into the narrow space around his mouth and nose. It seemed to cling to him with gentle fingers, pressing close against him in a soft blanket.

He hoped the end of him would be the end of the anger that burned so brightly in Jackie's eyes. Her father would see it as justice, final judgment for the man who had taken his son. More than anything, his mind filled with one final longing— to see Jackie look at him without bitterness in her eyes, with the gentle soul he knew still lived inside her somewhere.

"Lord, please take care of Jackie," he whispered, as the snow gobbled up the last of the precious air pocket. He closed his eyes and waited, surprised when he felt a vibration above him. The frozen mass around him undulated and shuddered. Another avalanche? The mass must have broken free, resettling before it carried him to oblivion.

His body continued to fight for life even in the face of the truth. His oxygen-starved lungs gasped for air, and he took in a mouthful of suffocating snow. Lungs burning, he choked against the cold that seared his throat, the frozen fire that spread inside him. The pain was overwhelming.

He tried to cough but there was no way to inhale. Drowning in snow. The end.

Then he felt someone pull his arm free and suddenly he was blinking against a wave of cold air, his chest heaving in an effort to inhale. He opened his eyes, momentarily blinded by a flashlight beam. Slowly Jackie materialized into view, her cheek close to his mouth, checking for breath.

When she straightened, her face was so stricken, so intense. He tried to speak, but his labored breathing wouldn't allow it.

She collapsed next to him. "Oh, Roman."

He managed to hold out a hand, which she grasped tightly. "I'm okay," he croaked somehow. "You found me in time."

"Thank you, God." Jackie clung to his hand and pressed it to her heart. "Thank you, God."

He tried to wrap his arms around her, to ease the fear she must have felt wondering if she was saving his life or recovering his body. His legs were still pinned under a pile of snow and he was too weak to yank them free.

Jackie moved away and used her shovel to dig him out.

He began to shiver uncontrollably.

She pulled a small tarp from her pack and spread it on the snow. His legs felt like rubber, refusing even to help him to sitting position. Jackie grabbed hold of his jacket and slid him onto the tarp. Then she took out a tightly rolled wool blanket, unfurled it and put it around his shoulders.

His shivers turned to full-blown shudders. "So cold."

"Your lips are blue. You're hypothermic. Fallon's gone to get help." She sat down next to him, pulled off her ski cap and slid it onto his head. Then she unzipped her jacket, pulled him into her arms and wrapped the wool around them both. She pressed her face to his neck.

He closed his eyes and hung on, letting her warmth seep into his body. His mind was scattered. The avalanche, his close encounter with death seemed far away, as if they belonged in some kind of dream, or nightmare. The only thing that penetrated his fog was the feel of Jackie, tucked in his arms, her face lying against his throat. He had a vague sense that the moment would not last, but he sank down and savored it.

They waited in darkness. He did not know how much time had passed when Fallon and Dax arrived with a Rescue Boggan hitched to the back of Dax's snowmobile. He tried to refuse.

I don't need help. I'm okay. The words refused to come out and his legs still wouldn't cooperate. Jackie and Dax each grabbed one of his arms and hauled him to the toboggan, strapping him inside and zipping the nylon covering around his lower body.

Jackie draped the wool blanket over him again. She leaned down and pressed her lips to his temple. "We'll get you to a hospital."

"No," he managed.

She cracked a smile. "I know, I know. You're fine."

He watched her climb onto the back of Fallon's snowmobile, and then began the bumpy descent down the mountainside. Every small groove in the snow sent a wave of pain through him, jarring his bruised body all the way back to the lodge. He didn't care. He looked up at the dark sky glittering with a thousand stars and he thanked God for letting him live.

Jackie paced back and forth down the hallway. "This is ridiculous. We should be getting someone to fly him to the hospital."

Dax nodded and stifled a yawn. "Yeah, but he wouldn't go even if there was anyone available, which there isn't because

Jimmy has an engine out and Doug's at the hospital waiting to give Skip a lift back. Good thing we had a doctor check into the Glacier cabin this morning. At least he's got some kind of care."

She folded her arms in exasperation. "He's been through an avalanche and probably has hypothermia."

The bedroom door opened and a tall man with a handlebar mustache stepped out. "You're right, he does have hypothermia. It's moderate, I'd say. His body temp dropped to 89.9 degrees, but I think we've got it on the upswing. Keep applying the warm bottles of water to his chest, and when he's awake give him lukewarm sweet tea. He's young and strong, so I think he'll make a complete recovery if he cooperates. Come get me if he takes a turn."

"What about Fallon?"

The doctor chuckled. "I got enough teenage attitude from her to let me know she's just fine."

Dax nodded. "She was sound asleep when I brought a sandwich to her room earlier. I left it on the table."

Jackie thanked the doctor as he left to return to his cabin. "Dax, how is June?"

"Stable. I called and told Skip you'd found Fallon. He's going to come back late tonight and take her to see her mom."

In spite of her fatigue, Jackie straightened. "Okay. You go get some sleep. You've been trying to do everything around here. I'll stay with Roman and keep him following doctor's orders." She firmly vetoed Dax's refusal. "Go, Dax. Skip and June are going to need you to keep things on track here, and you can't do that if you run yourself down. Go. I'll call you if I need something."

He nodded and disappeared down the hallway.

Jackie crept into the room where Roman lay on the bed, covered in blankets. He slept, head turned to the side, hair falling in his eyes, a series of scratches and bruises on his face.

She pulled a chair next to him and gently brushed the hair away. The warmth of his skin felt so different from the nearly frozen body she'd frantically dug out of the snow.

He'd been seconds away from death. If it had taken her one more moment to find the cord, if Fallon hadn't been there to help guide her…

Without warning, tears flowed down her cheeks. She sat back and pressed a tissue to her face to muffle the sound. What was this crazy storm of emotion coursing inside? Roman was a man she had felt only anger toward for two long years, so why had his brush with death unraveled her self-control?

Jackie had a desperate desire to talk to Asia. Her best friend was a whiz at all things emotional. She smiled, in spite of her tears, picturing how happy Asia had been since she and Mick got together. They seemed so right for each other.

Jackie glanced at Roman. They had been that way too, once upon a time. So why did the mere thought of him buried under the snow make her stomach quiver? Just common concern, she thought, the same way you'd feel about any poor wretch almost buried alive under an avalanche. She had a feeling Asia would fix her with a penetrating look and say, "Get real, girlfriend."

To keep herself sane, Jackie tried to keep her thoughts on Asia as she paced the room. Surely her friend had had time to collect any proof she'd needed by now. Why hadn't she heard from her? She grabbed her phone and stepped into the hall, dialing Asia's number for what seemed like the millionth time. Still no answer.

A restless need to do something, anything to take her mind off the past few hours, prowled through her. With another glance through the door at Roman sleeping, she decided to retrieve her laptop from the cabin.

She threw on a jacket and headed for the door. The sky was dark and clouded, only a pale moon shining overhead. She shot a nervous look to the ridgeline, remembering the shot that had come out of nowhere. Lloyd's cabin was dark and she wondered what he'd been up to in the hours they'd been gone. Certainly not working on any articles, she thought ruefully. As quickly as she could manage without slipping on the new-fallen snow, she jogged to her cabin and let herself in.

Hunger pounced on her like an angry wolf as she passed the kitchen. There was nothing to eat there, so she grabbed her laptop and returned to the lodge, heading for the kitchen to fix herself a sandwich. She was relieved to find the fridge filled with egg casseroles ready to be baked up for breakfast and par-boiled potatoes that would be turned into a succulent side dish. After slapping together a quick ham-and-cheese sandwich, Jackie warmed a pitcher of water to refill the bottles keeping Roman warm under his pile of blankets.

Armed with her supplies and laptop, she was about to return to check on Roman when she noticed an envelope with her name on it tacked to the message board. A time scrawled on the front showed it had been delivered that morning. With a flicker of worry, she pocketed the note and made her way back.

Roman stirred and opened his eyes when she laid a hand on his forehead. His voice was hoarse. "Hey."

"Hey, yourself. How are you feeling?"

"Like a train ran over me."

She smiled. "That sounds about right. I'm going to refill your water bottle." He lifted his arm and she filled the container with warm water and put it back, her fingers grazing his chest. She was relieved once again to feel the warmth of his muscled shoulders as she replaced the bottle. She couldn't resist laying her palm against his chest to feel the reassuring thump of his heart.

When she withdrew, he grabbed her hand. "You saved me. Thank you."

She was captured by the look in his eyes. From the very core of her being she wanted to pull him close and feel his warmth against her body. His lips were tantalizingly close, eyes pools of warmth and security.

But things had not changed, had they?

He was the same Roman, and they still had her brother's death between them like a shadow that blotted out the sunlight. But something had shifted inside of her when she'd thought he was gone, a feeling that moved in a powerful wave like the whirling push of snow.

"You're welcome," she whispered.

His eyes closed in sleep again, and she settled down into a chair, taking deep breaths to try and calm the tingling of her nerves. She'd taken several bites of the sandwich when she remembered the note in her pocket.

With a feeling of dread, she tore open the envelope.

NINETEEN

Roman struggled to a sitting position and waited for the spinning in his head to stop. His ribs were aching and his knee was sore, but they seemed only minor inconveniences. He was alive, and he still found it hard to believe. He'd survived an avalanche, thanks to Jackie. She'd found him in the middle of a vast nothingness. He felt deep down in his gut that God was trying to tell him something.

She was asleep, her head resting on the small writing table. He looked at the soft shelf of hair that fell in a fiery wave over her shoulders and concealed her face. Why had she saved him? Why had she put her own life on the line to rescue him?

He wanted to gather her up, bury his face in her hair and wrap himself in her closeness.

As he slowly stood, he noticed a piece of paper on the floor at his feet. He managed to pick it up, in spite of a splitting pain in his skull.

> J,
> She'll be here tomorrow night. Wants your thumb-drive data so we can put our heads together. I'll meet you at the lodge to arrange.
> M

Roman's jaw clenched. It must be from Mick.

He was unsure what to do. The note obviously had not been intended for him to read, but he couldn't shake the suspicion that Asia and Mick were up to something, something danger-ous that Jackie refused to see. He folded the note and put it on the table next to her. Ignoring the aching in his limbs, he pulled on a spare pair of boots from the closet and his sweatshirt, which someone had draped over the chair to dry. There was a hole in the knee of his jeans, but that was a small price to pay after being swallowed alive by an avalanche. He was relieved to find his satellite phone on the bedside table. It had survived the avalanche, secure in his breast pocket, though it had cost him a large bruise on the chest.

He tucked the phone away and looked at Jackie's small form, draped over the table, and wondered again how she had had the strength to save him. And why God had made it happen? He experienced again the warmth, her warmth, bringing him back to himself. A spot inside that had lain still and silent since the moment Danny died seemed to fill with a savage new heat.

The noise of clanging pots and cheerful conversation greeted him as he made his way to the kitchen. Mrs. Vogel, a lady he knew from church, wrapped him in her plump arms and kissed him.

"You rascal. Going off and getting yourself avalanched. Shouldn't you be in bed?"

He smiled and gave her wrinkled cheek a peck. "I promise I won't do it again. At least for a while." He looked over her shoulder, amazed to find the dining hall crammed full of people. "What…?"

Mrs. Vogel poured orange juice into a large pitcher. "The lights."

Of course. He must still be foggy from the accident. It was the last Winterfest event. The big finale where people de-scended on the lodge for food and a presentation on the northern lights before they all snowmobiled to a prime location to watch the display.

"Skip back yet?"

"He should be momentarily, but I don't think he can be counted for much help today. We've got to run things without the Delucchis." She dished out a platter of fried potatoes. "And by the way, Wayne called and said you're not to fly today, in case you had any ridiculous notions about doing that."

"Great. I'm grounded." Though he had a strong desire to get the plane into the air and fly away so he could sort out the crazy events of the last few hours, part of him was relieved that he'd have the opportunity to keep a close eye on Jackie.

"Right. So if you're feeling up to snuff, you can take this to the hungry hordes."

An hour later, he'd just sunk down in a corner chair to eat some breakfast himself when Jackie came in. She looked bleary-eyed and worried.

"What are you doing up and around? The doctor told you to take it easy."

"I am taking it easy. I'm grounded from flying today so I'm helping out."

She shook her head in exasperation. "Stubborn."

He didn't answer. She made no mention of the note, but her eyes scanned the group.

"Looking for someone?"

Her brows knitted and he could see her turning it over, weighing whether or not to tell him after his criticism of her friends. "Mick left a note that Asia will be here tomorrow. He wants to meet me and talk about it. I know you have doubts about them, but when she gets here, you'll see."

He satisfied himself with a nod. She had trusted him enough to tell him about the note. It sent a warm feeling swirling inside his gut. "Thanks."

Jackie shot him a quizzical look. "What for?"

"For telling me about your meeting with Mick."

She looked down at her feet. "I do trust you, you know. In spite of everything that's happened." Suddenly, she reached out and brushed his shoulder with her hand. "Kind of scared me when you got yourself buried in a half ton of snow."

He experienced a river of warmth where her fingers touched him. "More like two tons."

She laughed. "Tonight is the northern lights excursion?"

"Yes." He had a flash of the three of them, Jackie, Danny and himself, experiencing the awesome spectacle. Jackie must have felt it too.

She shook her head after a moment. "I'll go see if they need any help in the kitchen."

Roman ate his breakfast and did an informal survey of the crowd. Lloyd was there. He seemed distracted, continually looking up from his meal. When he caught Roman's eye he hurried over.

"I heard from the lady in the kitchen what happened. You okay, young fella?"

Roman nodded. "Banged up, but okay."

Lloyd tamped down his mustache. "I looked everywhere I could think of for Fallon, but no luck. I hear she got back okay."

"Uh-huh. We appreciate your help. Must take a lot of time away from your writing."

Lloyd raised an eyebrow. "Not too much. I still meet my deadlines."

"What did you do before you became a writer, Mr. Lloyd?"

"Why do you ask?"

"Wondered, is all. I know you're from the San Francisco area, like Jackie."

Lloyd's eyes narrowed. "You're an observant one, aren't you?"

"I try to keep an eye on things."

"Does that include keeping an eye on me?"

"Definitely."

After Lloyd left, Roman snuck off to a corner with Wayne's laptop and spent another half hour poring over any information he could find on Byron Lloyd. He looked up to find Jackie next to him.

"I'm snooping again, so if you are going to get upset, let's get it over with."

She sighed and gave him a wan smile. "I'm too tired to throw a fit. And, besides, at least this will keep you still for five minutes."

He laughed and they crowded together to look at the screen. It didn't take long.

When the information popped up, Jackie closed her eyes. "So Byron Lloyd did more than manage Security Plus. He is a…"

"Private investigator," Roman finished.

As the morning ticked by, Jackie felt a strong urgency to run. Lloyd was a P.I. He'd been working for Reynolds all along, just as she suspected. Her gut told her to flee to town, retrieve the thumb drive and wait for Asia's arrival. She wanted nothing more than to hug her tight and reassure herself that her best friend was safe and well.

Her mind continued to construct a rough plan. In a matter of hours, Asia's plane would touch down in Alaska and they could put an end to the whole mess. Roman would take them to an Alaska state trooper and lay the whole thing out, set the wheels in motion for Dr. Reynolds's arrest and her life would return to normal.

Normal? What was normal anymore? Would she go back to her small apartment in San Francisco and find another job? The idea didn't cheer her. Maybe she should move to Maryland to be closer to her father. She thought of their last conversation.

He killed your brother. You should never forget that.

She knew she would never forget the accident. *But what about forgiveness?* The sound of Roman's deep voice played in her ears. The idea came in a flash, startling her. She'd prayed for Roman, prayed for his recovery from the accident in spite of her own hurt and anger, hadn't she? She'd done her part to be a good Christian. But she had never asked God to help her forgive him. She'd never really thought about taking that last step.

"Well, it's not the time to think about it now," Jackie muttered. The lodge was filled with people clutching coffee cups and settling in to hear the northern lights presentation. She moved to the kitchen, desperate to keep busy until Mick showed up to give her the scoop on Asia's arrival. Mrs. Vogel cast her a desperate look.

"You're an able-bodied person looking to help, I hope?"

"Yes, ma'am." Jackie took the stack of cardboard the woman held out to her.

"Good. I've got Roman putting napkins and the cookies into the boxes we've already assembled for the box dinners tonight. Only forty more to go," she said cheerfully.

Jackie was happy to move to the far side of the kitchen, away from Roman. Her mind was a mixed-up jumble and she wanted to preserve the space between them, but the image of him buried under the snow made her heart flutter. The feel of his breath on her neck, proof that it was not too late, replayed in her mind, giving her a chill.

It was delayed shock from the avalanche. That was all. She busied herself folding the flat cardboard into small dinner-boxes that would accompany the guests on their last Winterfest event. When she was finished, Mrs. Vogel handed her a platter of wrapped sandwiches to add to the boxes. She was forced to move closer to Roman so they could complete the box-stuffing together.

He gave her a long look. "I've got to talk to you about something."

"Are you going to see the Lights?"

"Not sure. Are you?"

She was about to reply when they heard the shout. "No, I won't go."

A door slammed and Skip made his way into the kitchen. His forehead was creased with worry and his face heavy with fatigue. Mrs. Vogel hugged him and pressed a cup of coffee into his hand. The three gathered around as he sank into a chair.

Jackie squeezed his shoulders. "Is June doing well?"

Skip sighed. "At the moment. They're going to do a procedure on her to repair some internal damage to an artery. They feel confident it will go okay. Doug flew me back to bring Fallon to see her mom, but she won't go." He leveled his gaze at Roman and Jackie. "What happened when you found her? Dax told me some of it. I'm so grateful none of you were seriously injured."

Mrs. Vogel discreetly moved away to tend to the loaves of bread ready for baking.

Roman told Skip about finding Fallon at the cabin.

Skip rubbed his forehead. "Why'd she go there?"

Jackie hesitated. "She was hoping Mick would give her a ride to the airport, but he refused so she holed up there."

"She is so hardheaded. She just won't see the reality of it."

Roman lifted an eyebrow. "Of what?"

Skip shook his head. "Never mind."

The same strange look passed over his face, the one he'd had after Roman saved him from falling after the forklift accident.

Roman shoved his hands into his pockets. "Maybe I shouldn't bring it up now, but she said that you and June have been lying to her and she somehow feels that Danny's death is her fault."

He jerked. "What? Did she tell you why?"

"No."

Skip stared at Roman and then stood abruptly. "I've got to go."

Jackie couldn't restrain herself from asking, "Do you know why she feels responsible for Danny's accident?"

Skip shook his head. "No idea. Even though I know it's a useless effort, I'll talk to her again. I'm going back to the hospital and I'll try to be here to help with the viewing, but no guarantees. I hate to ask it, but…"

Roman held up a hand. "No need to ask. I volunteer. I'll ride over with the guests and supervise the event."

Jackie frowned. "You shouldn't be doing that after what you've been through."

He shrugged, and she knew he'd made up his mind, so she gave in. "I'll go too."

Skip sagged in relief. "Warn them about the bluff. I'll leave light sticks to mark the edge so nobody gets too close. The last thing I need is for one of the guests to take a header." He started back toward Fallon's room.

Jackie didn't think he was going to have any better result talking to Fallon the second time. Still she had the sense that Skip had not told them everything, and she saw the curious frown on Roman's face as he watched Skip depart.

TWENTY

Roman had the vague notion that Jackie was keeping away from him intentionally. Part of him didn't mind. The feel of her next to him, pulling him back from that deathly freeze, kept flooding his senses. He owed her his life, and he didn't like the feeling.

Of all the people in the world to rescue him, it had been Jackie.

Just the thought of her threw him into a storm of feelings he didn't want to indulge. Why had they been drawn together in this strange time, when he'd finally been able to push her from his heart and get a grip on the painful memories of Danny that plagued him? Why now?

He had no good answer, so he focused on piling the boxes into the snowmobiles and helped the two dogsledders who had arrived load their packs. He moved on to assist Dax in clearing snow from the walkways, working against his aching muscles, which groaned in protest. Mrs. Vogel recruited him to serve lunch and an afternoon snack. All the while he tried to keep a lookout for Mick. The guy had promised to arrive for his meeting with Jackie, but there had been no sign of him. *Just as well,* Roman thought. *I want to be right in the mix when he does show up.*

Before Roman knew it, it was time to ready the adventurers for the journey.

The best viewing would occur between 10:00 p.m. and 2:00

a.m., and their departure from the lodge should happen shortly after the dinner break. It was only about a three-hour trek, including stops for picture-taking. Fortunately, the sky was clear as the fifty-some visitors assembled in front of the lodge.

Over the whine of two dozen snowmobiles and the excited yap of the sled dogs, Roman tried to catch sight of Fallon. Had Skip successfully convinced her to go see her mother? He hoped so. He knew with painful clarity how soon things can end and the hurt of losing someone with no chance to say goodbye. The memory poked at him again, the strange detail he'd recalled while buried under the snow. A shadowy figure watching the accident. It must have been the product of carbon dioxide poisoning. Or the first glimmer of memory returning? Still, it left an uneasy feeling in his gut.

As he distributed the last of the boxed meals, Roman saw Lloyd motor up on a snowmobile. He was red-cheeked, as if he'd been hurrying to make it to the group before departure.

"Hello, young fella. You in charge of this party too?" Lloyd's face gave away nothing of his secret.

"Yeah, I guess so. I didn't think you were into sightseeing, Mr. Lloyd."

"I'm a man of mystery, don't you know." He smiled.

"So I've heard." Roman did not return the smile. The guy did know how to handle a snowmobile, he noted. Finally, Dax joined in on his machine with Jackie on the back. She looked distracted, her gaze flicking through the crowd. He caught her eye, but she looked hastily away.

He got the group quieted down, gave directions to the first stopping point and joined the head of the pack. Jackie and Dax would bring up the rear to ensure no one got lost. The moon was perfect for viewing the lights. It left the group with only the illumination from their snowmobile headlamps for navigation. They began their noisy trek, the visitors squealing with delight and calling to each other over the noise of the engines. He almost didn't notice the last snowmobile slide in at the periphery of the group, the rider sitting easily astride the seat, black hair curling from under his knit cap.

Mick had arrived after all.

Roman's job had just gotten harder.

Jackie tried to read the look on Mick's face for news of Asia, but it was a futile effort. They flew along, bumping over snow hills and concentrating to keep from banging into the visitors who had a tendency to stop and start without warning. She would just have to wait until they reached a stopping point.

The opportunity came an hour later when they came close to a sheltered snowy hollow, bathed in long shadow by the moon. Roman signaled the group to stop and the tourists readied their cameras, splitting into groups to take pictures of the distant mountain and the white-capped trees. An owl flew down, settling in a treetop to the thrill of the crowd. Several moments later they were equally enthralled at the progress of an arctic hare, hopping on its huge rear legs, peering with luminous eyes at the people.

Jackie didn't have to look long for Mick. He grabbed her elbow and pulled her to the shelter of a nearby spruce.

"Dax told me about the avalanche. You okay?" His dark eyes gleamed in the darkness.

She nodded. "Yes, but that was a close one. When will Asia be here?"

"She's finally got an evening flight in tomorrow."

"Did she find the proof she was looking for?"

His face was grim. "Yeah. Reynolds locked her out of the computer system but she managed to scrape together enough to combine with the data she sent you. Have you got it?"

"It's in the bank. I can get it out tomorrow."

He nodded thoughtfully. "Good. The sooner we hand this over to someone, the better off we'll all be."

"Is Asia okay? Why hasn't she called me?"

He shook his head. "Didn't want to involve you any further, maybe? Who knows? She's a stubborn one."

Jackie laughed. "Yes, she is. She refused to go out with you for two months."

He grinned. "I know. I thought maybe she'd heard that you turned me down."

Jackie's cheeks warmed. "No, no, I just wasn't ready to start dating again." After losing her brother and Roman, she didn't think she'd ever be ready again. Besides, Mick was not her type. She wanted a quiet man, steady, reliable, strong and gentle at the same time. She wanted someone like…Roman? Her heart lurched and she tried desperately to shake the thought away.

Mick didn't seem to notice. "I had to pull out all the stops for Asia. I think it was me in a tux on Valentine's Day with long-stemmed roses that finally did it. Imagine, being able to refuse my charm for that long?"

Thinking about her friend in happier times boosted Jackie's sense of hope. Maybe there really was an end to the madness. "So how will we arrange this?"

"I'll meet you in town tomorrow and we'll figure out exactly what flight she's arriving on. Then we'll go from there."

The thought of having her friend safe and the whole mess over with brought tears to her eyes. Mick peered closely at her and wrapped her in a hug.

"I'm sorry about all this, Jackie. It's going to be over soon. Promise."

Jackie heard a loud cough and she looked up to find Roman standing there, holding out a flashlight.

"Thought you might need an extra. I heard you say you're going to town tomorrow, Jackie. I'll fly you." He flicked a glance at Mick. "Did you want a lift too?" There was a challenge in the tilt of his chin, his scratched and bruised face showing no sign of good humor.

"No need. I'm getting really good at getting around this hunk of nowhere."

Jackie saw Roman open his mouth to retort so she interrupted. "Asia's coming tomorrow. I need to go to the bank in the morning to retrieve the data she sent me. I'd appreciate a flight, if it isn't too much trouble."

Roman nodded. "No trouble at all. I've got three guests to drop at the airport so there's room."

Mick's eyes narrowed but he said nothing.

"Thank you."

Dax called Roman over to help tinker with one of the snowmobiles.

A bundled tourist approached with camera flashing, followed by several more in search of the perfect picture. Jackie gave Mick a little wave and moved back to join the group. She knew he was angry that she'd let Roman in on Asia's arrival plans.

Mick's state of mind didn't ruin her sense of anticipation. She was almost overwhelmed by the relief of it all. Soon it would be over. Soon she would have her life back.

And soon she could leave Alaska for good.

Sadness washed over her as she watched the unending black sky, glowing with a glitter of stars. Roman stood, tall and commanding, silhouetted against the luminous snow behind him. He was looking at her and she wondered what he felt. Did he have the same inexplicable feeling inside? A mixture of wonder, fear and longing?

It was shortly after ten. They were about a mile from the viewing site when Roman took off ahead of the pack. He arrived at the overlook and set out the light sticks to mark the edge. The quiet was intense, broken only by the sound of a wind whispering across the snow. The northern lights danced their ballet over his head.

He'd seen them countless times before, but his heart quickened anyway at the undulating ribbons of green and blue. Scientists thought the phenomenon was caused by solar winds flowing across the earth's upper atmosphere, hitting molecules of gas and lighting them up like neon signs. Alaska Native legend said that the lights were flaming torches carried by departed souls, guiding travelers up to heaven.

He'd often yearned to float up into that whirl of color, to let go of the sin and guilt that plagued him and meet God, face-to-face and forgiven. He wondered how it would feel to let down the heavy burden he'd carried for two years, like a cold stone imbedded in his heart.

His thoughts were interrupted by the arrival of the group. When the noisy throng approached, he stopped them.

"The display varies from night to night, but it looks like we've got perfect conditions tonight."

"Are they dangerous?" a woman in a fur hat asked.

"No, ma'am. An intense display can cause problems with electric power lines and disrupt shortwave communication. They've also zapped an occasional satellite, but I think we're safe. Just steer clear of the edge here. There's a thirty-foot drop." He pointed to the row of light sticks. "Other than that, enjoy the northern lights."

He was surprised to see Skip offering photography tips to the visitors.

"When did you get here?"

"About two miles ago. I got a flight back and caught up with you. Going okay so far?"

"Haven't lost anyone yet. How is June?"

Skip smiled. "She came through the procedure just fine. I

managed to get Fallon to come with me. She's with her mom now. Staying there until the morning."

Roman sighed. "Good. Glad to hear it." Though he wanted to press more about Fallon's odd comments, he decided it was not the time. He caught sight of Jackie standing slightly away from the group, her face lifted to the streaming colors. The reflections danced in her eyes and the emotion on her face took his breath away. He allowed himself to experience again the pull he'd felt toward this amazing woman with the lights in her eyes.

TWENTY-ONE

Jackie stood under the shimmering colors, lost in a swirl of memory. She'd taken the camera, stolen it really, after Danny had told her not to.

I saved two summers of allowance for that camera and you're not touching it. Got it?

She'd taken it anyway, when he had been ice fishing with their father, and hiked with Roman to a good spot to photograph the northern lights. She'd felt then as she did now, overwhelmed by the sparkling display, sucked into a phenomenon that could only be God breathed. They'd stayed, taking picture after picture, until finally they had laid down on their backs in the snow and watched, real Alaska Native style, until the lights vanished back into heaven.

She hadn't realized the camera had fallen out of her pocket until she'd found it, lens cracked, on the snow. She'd hiked home and confessed to Danny with a sense of dread.

He was mad, frustrated, and then a roguish smile broke through the anger. She could see that smile so clearly, the sparkle in his eye, the wide grin.

All right. I forgive you, sis, but next time you swipe a camera, take my old one.

It was as if he was standing next to her, his arm draped around her shoulder.

I forgive you.

It was one of the most remarkable things about her brother; he could not hold a grudge, nurse any anger or hang on to old hates.

I forgive you.

She wished that the same glorious spirit of forgiveness would fill her soul. The realization came to her in a flash. Forgiveness was the light that would shine inside and push away the sooty anger that clung to her heart.

Danny would have forgiven Roman for the accident, she knew with a bolt of clarity, like he'd forgiven her for the camera.

Danny would have forgiven because he was a mirror that reflected love back to people, even people who had wronged him.

She wanted to raise her arms up to the light. The verse echoed in her mind.

> Though your sins are as scarlet,
> They will be as white as snow.
> Though they are red like crimson,
> They will be like wool.

She knew then that she needed to ask the Lord to forgive her for the anger and hatred she'd fostered toward Roman.

He would forgive her, and she would do the same for Roman.

A comfort bubbled up inside that she hadn't felt in a very long time. It sparkled and twirled inside her heart like the lights frolicking across the sky.

Her concentration was broken by an arm on her shoulder. She yelped and turned to find Roman, the colors reflected in shifting shadows on his face.

"You okay?"

She swallowed. "Yes. I really am." She looked again at the sky. "The perfect viewing night."

His sigh was soft. "I've always thought it was perfect out here at night, northern lights or not."

They watched a brilliant twist of neon-green light up the sky. The visitors bustled around them in the darkness, gasping in astonishment.

She surprised herself by taking Roman's hand. "I, I remember so many visits to the lights, with you." She squeezed his fingers. "Those were good memories for me, and Danny. I just wanted you to know that. Being here has made me rethink a lot of things. I think I've spent too long being angry."

His hand gripped hers and she thought she saw a gleam of moisture in his eyes. He cleared his throat. "You had the right."

"Yes, I had the right to be angry, but I also had the choice to forgive, and I didn't."

He closed his eyes for a moment. He opened his mouth to speak when Lloyd approached. "Sorry to intrude."

Jackie could not pretend civility to this imposter for one second more. "Why are you investigating me?"

She saw him look to see if anyone was listening. A reckless hum of anger filled her.

"I don't know what you mean, young lady."

Roman spoke from behind them. "Yes, you do. You're a private investigator and you were probably hired by Reynolds to come here. Why?"

Lloyd pursed his lips. "This isn't a very good time to discuss it. It's kind of public."

"I don't care." Jackie's voice trembled. "I want to know the truth. Are you working for the crime ring? The one Reynolds has been feeding patient information to? Are you here to shut me up?"

He blinked and stepped closer to them. The words came out, low and startling. "I should be asking you the questions."

* * *

Roman should have looked to see if anyone was within earshot of Jackie's confrontation with Lloyd, but he was beyond caring about propriety. After Lloyd's statement she backed up and into him. He could feel her body shaking as he steadied her. "Why would you say something like that to Jackie?"

"Because, young fella, Dr. Reynolds has been desperate to find out who is using his medical ID number and patient information illegally. There are only a few people with access to that kind of info and Jackie here is one of them."

"What?" Jackie gasped.

Lloyd went on. "Makes perfect sense. You had access to the files. So did your friend Asia and maybe she shared with her boyfriend, Mick. Whoever is involved, they've given private information to an organized crime ring that has used it to make millions. We haven't located Asia yet, but I was already tailing you when you cooked up this plan to fly away to nowhere, so I followed you."

"You broke into my cabin."

"I like to think of it as letting myself in. You're clever, I have to admit. I didn't find anything on your computer to link you to the crime. I was about to fly home and go after Asia, but then Mick showed up, so I figured sooner or later she'd come here, or at least contact you."

"I didn't do anything wrong." Her voice broke as she spoke. "Reynolds is the one stealing patient identities. He's trying to shift the blame to me."

Lloyd's eyes narrowed. "The man is a cardiologist, and you are a clerk. Which of you has the greater need to steal?"

Roman moved around Jackie and took a step closer to Lloyd. "Jackie didn't steal anything. You are the one lying here. Maybe Reynolds did send you—not to investigate, but to silence the people who could put him in jail, to destroy any evidence Jackie's collected. Could be you were the one who shot Jackie."

Lloyd shook his head. "It wasn't me. I deal in information, that's all."

Jackie's shoulders started to tremble more violently. Roman tried again. "If Reynolds was so suspicious, why didn't he go to the cops?"

"He tried that several years ago when this happened in another office of his, but the crime ring is too difficult to crack. Police got nowhere. This time he's decided to find the source of the leak. He knew he'd have much better results doing some digging than the cops."

Jackie's voice was faint. "I don't know what to believe."

Lloyd fixed them with a look that was devoid of any charm. "You can believe this, Miss Swann. If you are in possession of any patient data, you're going down. If there is any link to connect you to this crime, I'll find it and you'll go to jail. All of you, if necessary."

Lloyd turned on his heel, and Jackie sank to her knees.

Jackie felt Roman's arms around her as he lifted her and carried her to an empty blanket left by one of the guests. She noticed vaguely the hum and chatter of the admiring crowds as they watched the fantastic light spectacle, but it all seemed so very far away. She could not make sense of the encounter with Lloyd. It was all she could do to keep from screaming.

Roman knelt beside her. "Deep breaths." He squeezed her forearm.

"I don't understand," she croaked. "He thinks I'm responsible? Or Asia and Mick?"

"That is what he was saying, yes."

Her brain whirled. "Oh, Roman. Nothing makes sense anymore." Tears began to course down her face, freezing into icy trails.

He gently wiped them away. "You did what you thought was right at the time. Lloyd could be lying."

She took a breath, filled with a desperate need. She'd worked so hard to keep Roman out, to shield herself from relying on him. Now, she needed more than anything else to have his trust and to trust him as she had in the past. "I didn't steal anything. You believe me, don't you?"

His eyes were soft in the glow of the lights. She heard his quiet sigh. "Yes, Jackie. I do believe you."

She gripped both his hands. "Why? Why would you believe me? After all that's happened? With everything Lloyd said?" *After I cut myself off from you when Danny died?* "Tell me why you believe me."

He cupped her cold cheek. "Because I know you, Jackie. I've always known you and you are an honest person." He toyed with a strand of hair that had escaped her knit cap. "That's one of the things I fell in love with." He leaned forward and traced his fingers along both sides of her face and her lips.

Her stomach tightened and for a crazy moment, she wanted nothing more than to embrace him and press her lips to his. "Roman," she whispered and kissed him. Her lips just grazed his when he suddenly straightened and stood.

He cleared his throat. "We've got to get you to the police. Lay it all out for them before things get worse."

"No. I can't."

Roman fisted his hands on his hips. "Why not?"

"Because Lloyd is right. Medical theft is hard to prove. And I look guilty. We all do."

"But if we explain things…"

"Then I just live with the accusation hanging over my head and no one wants to employ me ever again." She tried to keep her breathing level. "Besides, I've got to talk to Asia first. She's coming in tomorrow."

She read the question in his eyes. "Asia is not a thief. She didn't have any more to do with this crime than I did, but she's got evidence to add to the data she sent me that will prove Reynolds did it."

She felt her cheeks warm thinking how she'd tried to hide the thumb drive from him.

He considered. "The police would be the best option. Let's say you're right and Mick and Asia aren't involved in any wrongdoing. I still don't think Lloyd is coming clean. He could be waiting for a chance to kill you and Mick and Asia when she gets here. Clean up the mess." He shook his head. "It's not worth the risk."

She stood and put her arms around his neck. "Please, Roman." She pressed her cheek to his. "I know I don't have the right to ask you to get mixed up in this, but I'm putting everything on the line. Please let me meet with Asia before we involve the police. I want to give her a chance to prove Reynolds guilty and save our reputations. She's my friend and I trust her. Please."

She felt the thrum of his pulse under his chin speed up, and his arms tightened around her. He held her close to his body, sheltering her from the cold. It felt so natural to be in his arms again. So perfect.

"All right," he said finally. "Only until Asia arrives."

The time had come to head back to the lodge. Roman and Skip collected the visitors and helped them rebundle their packs and prepare their vehicles. The dogs yapped in excitement, glad to be moving again after their long break. Roman made sure Jackie was safely on the back of Dax's snowmobile before he went to retrieve the light sticks from the ridge.

Skip stood, silhouetted against the sky. He held a light stick in his hand.

"Ready to go, Skip?"

He cocked his head in a bemused fashion. "Roman, are we missing someone?"

"Nobody has mentioned it. I'll take a head count."

Skip seemed mesmerized as he stared at the light stick.

Roman looked at him more closely. "What's wrong?"

"Look."

Roman joined him. The neatly spaced row of light sticks had been disturbed. Several were missing and the snow at the edge of the bluff was scraped away.

Fear ripped through him. Without a word, Skip and Roman drew as close to the edge as they could, slowly following the ridgeline, training flashlights down into the darkness.

He saw it after a few moments—one of the fallen light sticks acting like a tiny beacon, drawing his attention to the pile below. He must have made some exclamation because Skip shone his light at the spot.

The silence seemed to go on interminably until Skip blew out a breath.

"I guess we know who's missing now."

Byron Lloyd's lifeless body was a garish spot of color against the pristine white snow.

TWENTY-TWO

Roman wanted to tell Jackie privately, but the throng of people was beginning to get antsy, calling to Roman and Skip, eager to leave.

Skip turned away to phone the state troopers' office. "Gonna be a good four hours before they can get here. We can't have the guests stay out here that long."

Roman fought through the shock to piece together a course of action. "Take them back. Leave Dax with me and the Rescue Boggan. We'll try to disturb things as little as possible, but we've got to bring him up. He might still be alive."

The doubt in Skip's face matched the feeling in his gut. The twisted splay of limbs and the unnatural position of the neck told the hard truth. Byron Lloyd was dead.

Skip nodded. "I'll get them back, tell them there's been an accident and we'll wait for the troopers."

Roman nodded and remained at the ridge while Skip headed everyone in the direction of the lodge. The noise of engines and barking dogs soon faded into the distance as he gazed out over the precipice.

Dax trudged over, followed by Jackie.

Roman held out a hand. "Jackie, what are you doing here? You need to help Skip get everyone back to the lodge."

She raised her head a notch. "No. Something is going on. What happened? Tell me."

He sighed. There was no way he was going to get her to leave until she knew.

"It's Lloyd. He's fallen."

Her hands flew to her mouth. "Is he okay?"

Roman shook his head slowly. "No. I think he's dead."

Her mouth worked but no words came out.

He put an arm around her. "What we need to do right now is get him up here. There's a chance of snow and if he gets buried, we may never find him again. You need to stay here while Dax and I climb down and bring him up." He handed her the satellite phone. "You'll be the safety person. If there's trouble, call Skip and fill him in. Do you understand?"

She snatched the phone and gripped it. "Yes," she whispered. "I understand."

After another uneasy glance at her, he turned to Dax. "We can secure the ropes to the pine there. I'll go down, put him on the collapsible stretcher and yell when it's time to hoist him up."

Dax okayed the plan and removed coils of rope from his pack. He wrapped several lengths around the tree trunk and threaded the remainder over the edge of the bluff. "Want the climbing gear?"

"No. There's enough rock to get a foot into."

Dax looked down into the ravine. "Think he fell?"

"Do you?"

Dax shrugged. "Be a lot easier for everyone if he did."

Somehow, Roman didn't think anything about the situation would be easy.

He located the first rocky ledge and began his descent. The walls rose around him as he picked his way down, using the rope at the places where the footholds disappeared.

As he sought out the meager places to hold on to, he tried

to piece it all together. The guy had just accused Jackie and Asia of a crime. Now he was more than likely dead at the bottom of a ravine. He knew Jackie hadn't touched Lloyd. The fear in her eyes was now tempered by a deep trust she saw there, a trust in him. The moment sent a jolt through his heart.

She was desperate, that was all. In a dire predicament and he was the only person in her corner.

The situation had just gotten a whole lot worse, too. How would they keep the police out of the Dr. Reynolds business when they came to investigate Lloyd's death?

Perhaps no one had overheard Lloyd's accusations. It might have been merely a fall.

Then again, maybe someone had been listening.

And that same someone was guilty of murder.

Jackie watched Roman vanish over the icy edge. The cold ran through her in a frigid current, making her a part of the glacial terrain that stretched around them. Was it possible Lloyd had fallen? Was he so focused on his mission that he hadn't paid attention to where he was walking?

Lloyd was not—she swallowed—*had* not been a careless man. He'd broken into her cabin twice without being seen by anyone. He'd been able to watch her every move since she'd arrived in Alaska.

Had he reported each detail back to Reynolds? Did the doctor really think she and Asia were selling patient information? She clasped her arms tightly around herself. Lloyd had to have been lying. Reynolds was working for the crime ring, and Lloyd had been sent to quiet her. She remembered the shot that had come out of nowhere. The memory raised goose bumps on her skin.

Still, something was not right. Who killed Lloyd?

Get hold of yourself.

She longed for her brother's presence. He would have shared whatever load she had to shoulder willingly and faithfully, and so would…

Roman.

She wanted to run away from the truth, but she could not escape the fact that she was drawn ever closer to him. Something was changing inside her. The mountain of anger and resentment toward him was eroding away like the edge of an iceberg buffeted by a stormy sea. She felt the good memories, the happy moments they'd shared fill her. *Forgive.* The word danced in her mind, gently as the snow that had begun to fall.

Forgive.

The ringing of her satellite phone made her jerk. Mick's worried voice charged through the unit.

"Whew. Thank goodness you answered. I got to the turnoff and watched all the others head to the lodge, but you weren't there. What happened? Are you stranded somewhere? Are you hurt?"

"No." She felt a lump in her throat. "Mick, I heard tonight that Byron Lloyd is a private detective. He said Dr. Reynolds hired him to find evidence to pin the identity theft on us."

"What? You've got to be kidding me. He's lying. Don't trust him, Jackie. He's in league with Reynolds, I bet."

Jackie tried to interrupt his commentary. "Mick, listen. There's something else."

"I don't see how it could be worse. What?"

"Lloyd is dead. He fell, or was pushed, over the edge at the northern lights."

There was a long pause. "Unbelievable. This is like some bad movie or something. Is that where you are now?"

"Yes. Roman is bringing him up. Skip called the state troopers and they are going to come when they can. He's trying to keep the guests at the lodge until they arrive."

"That explains why he tried to get me to stay. I'm not into group camping. I had to get back to my cabin."

She sighed. "What are we going to do?"

"Follow the plan. When the cops arrive, tell them the truth. You don't know what happened to Lloyd. He might have fallen after all."

She watched the stretcher slide over the ledge, Dax hauling on the ropes. Her stomach heaved. "I don't think so."

Mick spoke more forcefully. "We're at the end of this, Jackie. By tomorrow the whole thing will be in the hands of the police anyway and they can put the pieces together, and figure out who killed Lloyd, too. Only a few more hours."

"I just can't understand why Asia hasn't called."

"As my father said too many times to count, 'Don't give up the ship.'"

"I'm trying."

"It works for the navy, it will work for us. I'll come and get you. I can be there in no time."

She smiled. "No, Mick. I'm okay here. I'll see you in town tomorrow. When?"

"Her flight's not in until three. Can you meet me at the airport beforehand?"

She tried to keep the quaver out of her voice. "If the police are done with me by then."

"Remember..."

"I know, I know. Don't give up the ship." She disconnected as Roman gingerly crested the top of the ridge, puffing in the cold night air. She wanted to help him, but her feet were rooted to the spot. Instead she watched as they moved Lloyd's body from the stretcher to the Rescue Boggan, zipping the black covering closed around his still form. Roman folded the stretcher and came to meet her.

His cheeks were flushed from the exertion, eyes dull from

fatigue. It occurred to her that he must be suffering from the battering he'd taken in the avalanche. She wanted to reach out to him, to tell him how sorry she was for involving him in the whole sordid mess. She brushed the snowflakes from his hair.

He gave her a tired smile. "I think we can go back now. I took pictures of the site as best I could for the troopers."

She nodded. "That rescue can't have been easy, especially since you're banged up."

He kissed her hand, sending tingles up her arm. "I'm tough."

"Yes, you are."

The awkward silence ended when Dax fired up his snow-mobile, the Rescue Boggan and its gruesome load attached to the back. "Storm's coming in. Best to go."

Roman climbed onto the other machine and Jackie slid on behind him. She held on tight as they sped toward the lodge. Time blurred into an endless moment of snow, darkness and fear. The only comfort was the feel of Roman's strong back, the movement of his muscles against her cheek as he guided them back to Delucchi's.

The lodge was quiet when they arrived just before sunup. Dax pulled the Rescue Boggan under the sheltered garage. The three of them made their way into the kitchen. Mrs. Vogel had not started on the breakfast preparations, but she'd left one of the giant metal thermos containers filled with hot coffee for them.

Shedding coats and hats, they sat down and poured the coffee, warming their hands on the thick ceramic mugs.

Skip joined them. "Got most everybody bunked in. Some weren't too happy about staying, especially after I heard that they can't get a trooper out here until afternoon. A cargo plane crash a hundred miles from here is taking all available personnel, and the approaching storm isn't helping. They said they'd get here when they could." He looked at Roman. "Did you…?"

"Yes, we photographed everything and brought him back."

Skip nodded. Jackie thought he looked a decade older than he had before June's stroke. She felt overwhelmingly guilty at adding to his burden by bringing Lloyd to the Delucchi Lodge.

He looked uneasily at Roman. "Look, I know we're supposed to stay here, but I can't leave June and Fallon alone much longer. I hate to ask it, Roman, but can you fly me to town? I'd wait for Jimmy, but I'm anxious to get back."

"I'll take you, if Dax can handle things."

Dax nodded. "Reg is back in action, and he should be here soon. Mrs. Vogel can handle the cooking and I heard her daughter is coming to help today too."

Roman shot Jackie a look.

She tried to sound nonchalant. "I'll come too."

Skip hesitated for a moment. "Okay, I guess. We can check in town to see if there's a safety officer back from the accident who can talk to us. The troopers can't expect us to stop everything until they arrive."

Jackie thought that they might expect exactly that, but she didn't say so. The delay in the troopers' arrival was a pure stroke of luck. She might just be able to get the thumb drive and meet Asia to straighten the whole thing out before she had a face-to-face with the police. They could put the pieces together, prove Reynolds was dirty and get their lives back.

She looked out the window as the blackness lifted from the horizon.

Hurry up, sun.

She thought about Lloyd lying dead in his dark cocoon. Though he'd been her enemy, sadness licked at her heart. He did not deserve to be murdered. No one did.

She couldn't stop from wondering.

If he was telling the truth about the shooting, the gunman was still very much on the loose. Who was he? And where was he?

TWENTY-THREE

Roman went to do the precheck on the plane. Jackie stayed in the kitchen to help Mrs. Vogel until he was ready to fly them out.

He wasn't surprised when Wayne called.

"Heard the call over the police band. You lost someone over the bluff?"

"Yes. Byron Lloyd."

Wayne grunted in surprise. "Any chance he fell?"

Roman sighed. "I suppose there's always a chance."

"But you don't think so."

"I don't know what to think. I'm flying Skip into town to see June, and Jackie is coming too. We left word for the police."

"Best you can do." He paused. "I remembered about the Arizona thing."

"What?"

"You said Fallon was looking at flights to Avondale. I remembered why I know that name. The girl that worked for the Delucclis when they first got things off the ground, she was from Avondale. Left town ages ago, maybe sixteen years or so. You and your ma hadn't come to live here yet."

Roman frowned. "Maybe my brain is full, but I can't figure out a connection right now. Fallon would have been too young when the woman left to remember her."

"I just relay the info and leave the connections to you. I need to get back to work, but if I can be of help, let me know. You'd better get that bird in the air. Storm is coming in harder. May be grounded if it kicks up."

"Yeah. See you later." He put the newest tidbit out of his mind. Things were bad and soon to be worse. Roman knew Wayne was right. The situation with Dr. Reynolds was far from over, and he was still smack in the middle of it. He hadn't noticed himself getting entangled in Jackie's life again, and never would have guessed he'd allow himself to be. But here he was, flying her to get proof to convict her boss, fully intending to stand with her until the entire thing was laid at the feet of the police department.

He identified the feeling that had nestled in his gut. Contentment. In spite of finding a dead man, of worrying about whoever was targeting Jackie, the mess with June and Fallon's emotional upheaval, he was content to be with Jackie again. He would never wash his memory of the awful grief he'd caused her, but for now, he was ridiculously pleased to have her close to him. He would see her through it safely if it was humanly possible. Then his heart would crawl back into its shadowed cave as he watched her fly away. He grabbed a tool kit and turned his attention to the engine.

Jackie and Skip walked over, their faces grave.

"Ready to take her up?"

Roman hadn't seen Skip so haggard before. He held a laptop under his arm. When he saw Roman glance at it, he shrugged. "It's Fallon's. We took it away from her because we didn't trust the places she was surfing. I'm going to take a close look at her search history and find out exactly who she's been contacting."

"Do you think she was going to fly to Arizona to meet someone?" Roman hesitated a moment. "Wasn't there a lady from Avondale who worked here when you first built the lodge?"

Skip held up a hand. "Fallon barely knew her. It doesn't matter, anyway. It's over now. Let's go."

Roman exchanged a puzzled look with Jackie. They boarded the plane and Roman rolled to the end of the runway before lifting off into the gray sky.

Jackie sat next to him, staring out the window.

He put a hand on hers. "You okay?"

She gave him a sad smile, her voice low. "I was just thinking and praying, about the choices I've made. I wish I could go back and change some of them."

He squeezed her fingers. "Don't go there, Jackie. There's only heartbreak down that road."

Her eyes were so full of tender emotion, he had to turn away.

Just keep her safe, Roman. He repeated the mantra again and again until he touched down at the airport and secured a van to get them to town. He dropped Skip off at the hospital.

"We'll come by later," Jackie called after him. He nodded distractedly and ran toward the entrance, head bowed against the driving snow. "I wonder what is really going on with Fallon. Do you suppose she met a boy online?"

Roman shrugged. "I don't know, but it seems like both Skip and June were aware that Fallon was searching for someone." He told her about the picture of the woman he'd seen in Fallon's room and Wayne's information.

Jackie frowned. "Fallon said they'd been lying to her all of her life."

The emotional scene at the cabin came back to him with painful clarity. Fallon blamed herself for Danny's accident.

It's their fault that I had to ask him. I couldn't figure out how to do it myself.

Jackie must have been recalling the moment too. "Roman, can you remember anything my brother said when he asked you to drive him to town? Did he mention doing a favor for Fallon?"

Roman took a deep breath and tried to comb the dark corridors of his memory. "If he did, I can't remember." His fists clenched in frustration.

She reached out a hand for his. "It's okay. When things simmer down with her mother, I'm going to need to get the truth out of her."

He wondered if learning Fallon's secret might allow him to finally put in order the terrible events that had happened that night. He glanced at Jackie, her delicate profile outlined by a thick braid of hair that seemed to catch the sunlight and glow like the twirling bands of northern lights. He didn't want to revisit that night. He was content to remain in this moment with her, close and without the anger.

She caught him looking at her. "Do you think about him often?"

He didn't need to clarify. "Yes. Every day of my life."

She was silent for a moment. "Me too. Before it was only angry, painful memories of losing him, but lately…"

Something stirred deep inside his gut. "Lately?"

"Since I came back here, I'm remembering the amazing times we had and the crazy, fun-loving person he was."

Roman felt the ever-present twist of pain. "Yeah, he was a great guy."

"Yes, he was, and I don't think he'd want us to dwell on the bad things." She clasped his forearm. "It's taken me a while to figure that out."

He felt the van closing in on him, the air sucked out until he couldn't breathe. He pulled away from her. "Jackie, I can't forget. I can't forget that I'm the one who killed your brother."

"I'm not talking about forgetting, I'm talking about forgiving."

"Your father will never forgive me," he said.

"Maybe not. That's his choice. I can only be responsible for my own." She eyed him close up. "The problem is, Roman, that you can't forgive yourself."

"I don't think I'll ever be able to do that."

He was relieved to pull up outside the bank. "Let's get this thing resolved."

She turned away and he knew he hadn't given her what she wanted or needed.

I'm sorry, Jackie.

His sin ran too deep, hurt too many people to be forgotten. Or forgiven.

The snow fell in a steady blanket as they parked. Jackie knew by the set of Roman's shoulders he didn't want to talk anymore. She didn't understand why she felt the strong compulsion to bring up the past. It would be easier to let things remain buried. Lately the whole world seemed to be tilted, her thoughts running on courses they'd never traveled before.

She tried to shake herself back to the present as she pushed through the door, wiping the snow off her jacket. Keeping her demeanor as normal as possible she asked to visit her safe-deposit box and retrieved the thumb drive. It felt like a live coal in her pocket. The time was just past eleven. The thought of waiting an agonizing four hours until Asia's arrival made her stomach churn. She wanted nothing more than to see her friend and get their lives back on track.

What would Roman do with his life after she left? Carry on his piloting duties? Buy the plane he'd always talked about and live in the small cabin close to the airport but far enough away from people not to feel crowded? He'd probably do just that. Maybe he'd meet some nice Alaskan girl to share his love of the outdoors. It would be a chance to make a fresh start with someone who did not remind him of the past.

Her stomach knotted and she wondered at her own reaction. She wanted to lift the terrible guilt that she'd helped to heap on his shoulders so he could find happiness, but the thought of him finding it in another woman twisted her insides.

"I've got to get out of this place," she muttered to herself, "before I forget who I am."

She found Roman standing under the eaves outside the bank, waiting.

He checked his watch. "Asia's plane isn't due for a while. Maybe we should go get some lunch."

She nodded and they walked to a tiny sandwich shop, filled with the scent of simmering pea soup. Roman purchased two sandwiches, sodas and bowls of soup and they settled in a corner table to eat.

It was a familiar place, the same scarred tables and roosterprint curtains they'd seen many times in her past visits. They'd talked for hours here, sometimes with Danny laughing and joking with them, and sometimes by themselves, talking about the future and planning their next adventure. She had not realized how very sweet those moments were. Looking at Roman's guarded face made them seem like far distant memories.

She'd made it through a half bowl of the succulent soup when her phone rang. Her heart ricocheted in her chest when she recognized Asia's cell number. "Hello, Asia? Is that you?"

There was no answer for a moment, until a faint voice whispered, "Jackie?"

"Yes, yes, it's me. Are you on your way?"

"I can't…"

A rumbling sound filled the line. "Asia? What's wrong?"

Asia started to answer, an urgent whisper that was abruptly cut off as the phone disconnected.

Jackie stared at the phone.

Roman had stopped eating and sat tense, waiting. "Asia?"

Jackie nodded.

"What did she say? Is she in the air?"

A blackness filled Jackie's vision and she fought to keep breathing. "She didn't really say anything, but her tone..." Jackie hurriedly called Mick's cell number. No answer. She slammed the phone down.

He reached across the table and took her hand. "What is it?"

"Probably nothing. I'm sure it's all in my mind." She blinked back the threatening tears. "I think I'm going crazy."

He squeezed her fingers. "One thing I've learned growing up here is you've got to trust your instincts."

She took a deep breath. "Roman, I've got a terrible feeling that something is very wrong."

He looked into her eyes for a long moment. "Tell you what. Come with me and we'll let Wayne, my boss, have a look at the thumb drive. I think you might have met him before. He's got an accounting background, and he's a friend, like a father, really. He's a good man. Trust me on this."

She saw the devotion in his eyes and she knew she trusted Roman with her life, but there was something else, deeper than trust and familiarity and shared history. With a shiver, she looked away.

TWENTY-FOUR

Roman introduced Wayne to Jackie as they settled into the worn chairs in his office.

Wayne smiled. "We may have seen each other a time or two when you came in the past, but I don't think we've ever officially met. Why don't you tell me the whole story and I'll see if I can help?"

Jackie shot Roman a look and he nodded encouragingly.

She related the course of events from the confrontation with Dr. Reynolds to the fake cop's visit to her apartment and on to the attack on Mick and her frantic flight to Delucchi Lodge. When she was done, she slumped in her chair. "I'm sure I've handled it all wrong. I'm so mixed up I can't think straight. I can't shake the feeling that something bad is going to happen to Asia if I don't figure it out."

"Let's take a look at that thumb drive." He took it from her and plugged it into his computer. "Give me a little while to poke around."

Roman led Jackie to the empty waiting area. They sat in cushioned chairs, facing the wide windows so they could see the planes lined up, ready for passengers. The snow had begun to collect on the ground in soft piles. When Jackie shivered, he wrapped an arm around her.

"Cold?"

She nodded. "Better now."

They remained like that for a while, watching the snow drifting down on the parked aircraft. He imagined himself flying his own plane. With a start he realized he pictured Jackie next to him in the passenger seat. When he looked down, he found her asleep, head against his chest.

He pressed a kiss to her forehead. "Oh, Jackie. How did we get here?"

Snuggling her tighter against his side, he allowed himself to savor the feeling of having her in his arms once again.

An hour later, Roman was startled awake when Wayne tapped him on the shoulder.

"Nap time's over, you two." He led them back to his office and Roman couldn't help but notice the grim expression on the man's face. His stomach tightened as he sat next to Jackie.

"There's a ton of information here that indicates part of your theory is correct. These claims are filtered through many different insurance companies and payments are laundered via a network of people. It's a sophisticated setup—definitely shows a crime ring is involved. The common denominator for all these claims is they all originated from Dr. Reynolds's office, using his license number."

Jackie sat rigid in the chair. "That's exactly what we've been thinking."

Wayne tamped down the corners of his mustache. "The question is, who shared the doctor's license number and patient info to be used by this crime ring."

Her voice was shrill. "What do you mean, who? Dr. Reynolds did."

Wayne shrugged. "That's one possibility."

Roman looked closely at his friend, dread pooling in his chest. "What's the other possibility?"

"Someone working at the office who had access to the information could be supplying it to the crime ring."

Jackie gasped. "That's what Lloyd said, but we didn't have anything to do with it."

Roman hated the desperation in her voice. "I know you didn't do anything wrong, Jackie. Is there any possibility at all that Asia is involved? Could she have been lying to you all this time?"

Her eyes were wild. "Why would she do that? If she was selling information, why bring the whole thing up to me in the first place? I might have never known if she didn't point it out. That's not something a guilty person would do."

Wayne paused. "Unless the guilty person knew they were under suspicion. Say, they got wind that Dr. Reynolds hired a private investigator and wanted to shift the blame by incriminating someone else."

"Me? I'm the office clerk, not the accounting person."

"Did you have access to the information?"

She stared. "Well, I suppose if I wanted to, I could have gotten into the system. But that would have been suspicious, wouldn't it? With people in and out all the time? With the doctor right there watching?"

Wayne raised an eyebrow. "Can you and Asia access your work accounts from home?"

The life seemed to leak out of her. She nodded miserably. "Yes, we both have office laptops so we can work from home on long weekends." Her hands began to shake. "So you think…you think Asia told me to take the drive so I would look guilty when Lloyd tracked me down?"

Roman leaned toward her. "He's just offering possibilities, thinking it through."

Wayne cleared his throat. "Couple other items I wondered about. These claims started the end of last February. When was Asia hired?"

Jackie blinked in concentration. "She started a year ago, December." Her face fell. "But there's a six-week training period. She didn't take over the position fully until…"

"Last February?" Roman finished for her.

She pressed her trembling lips together. "This can't be true."

Wayne pulled the thumb drive from the computer. "There's one more thing you should know."

Roman saw Jackie take a breath. "What?"

"Roman told me when we talked that Asia is supposed to arrive around three o'clock this afternoon."

Jackie twined her fingers together. "Yes."

"The last flight in today already landed at ten-thirty this morning. There is no three o'clock flight."

"She must have told Mick the wrong time, that's all. Maybe she's already here."

He shook his head slowly. "I did some checking and no one on the ten-thirty flight booked a hopper to the Delucchi Lodge or to any town nearby. I'm sorry, Jackie, but it seems like you've been lied to."

Her face crumbled and tears began to fall. Roman stood to put his hands on her shoulders. "I'm really sorry, honey."

Wayne put the thumb drive on the desk. His tone was gentle. "I can continue to dig around in this info, maybe shed some light on it for you."

She nodded miserably.

"In the meantime I'd be careful."

She turned a tear-washed face to him. "Because I look guilty?"

He didn't answer. "Let me know what else I can do."

Roman exchanged a look with Wayne before he left the room.

Jackie felt the disbelief ball up inside her in a fiery mass. She shot to her feet and began pacing the room. "This isn't possible. It doesn't make sense. Asia was scared. Mick was beaten up." She rounded on Roman. "What about that? How does that fit into Asia's evil plan?"

He stood to face her. "It's possible she arranged it, or maybe…"

Jackie's eyes blazed. "Or he's in on it too? Who's next? The copy-machine guy? Maybe Skip or June were paid off by this crime ring? This is getting ridiculous."

She stalked out of the office to the waiting area to give her body something to do. In the gathering gloom outside, a man brushed off the seat of a snowmobile and climbed on. The clock was inching toward two; it would be dark again soon. "None of this makes sense. I know her, I know Asia. She wouldn't be involved in this, she just wouldn't."

Roman trailed after her. "It's hard sometimes, when people betray you."

"That's just it, Roman. I'm sure she didn't do this. I'm going to call Mick. He got the flight information wrong. Maybe he can clear this up."

Mick would deal with the accusations.

Don't give up the ship, he'd say.

Her fingers searched for the phone in her pocket as a realization exploded in her mind with the force of a thrown grenade. Jackie's voice came out in a whisper as the coldness settled inside. "It can't be."

He turned a worried gaze on her. "What?"

The pieces fell into place with painful precision. She tried to answer him, but her mouth refused to cooperate. Her knees shook and she felt herself falling.

Roman helped her to a chair.

She pressed her hands to her mouth to keep from shouting. "It's impossible. How could I not have seen it before?"

He reached out a hand to her. "What is it?"

"I know who is behind all this."

Roman knelt next to her and waited.

"There was another person who could have gained access to the files the same time Asia did."

I had to pull out all the stops. I think it was me in a tux on Valentine's Day with long-stemmed roses that finally did it. Imagine, being able to refuse my charm for that long.

The man who had shown up at her apartment, impersonating a cop. Her neighbor had said he was an ex-Navy man. She'd leapt to that conclusion after seeing a tattoo of a ship on the man's arm. A tattoo honoring a long-dead father.

My dad was my hero, he'd said.

Jackie groaned. "Mick tried to date me when he first showed up. I refused. I didn't want to see anyone…" she dropped her gaze. "After you."

Roman pressed her shoulder. "Go on."

She took a deep breath. "He asked me out several times, but I brushed him off. Then he pursued Asia." She told him about the tattooed stranger at her apartment. "Mick was behind the whole thing, I'm sure of it."

"So he faked the attack on himself in San Francisco to make you think you had to run? Clever."

"Asia said there were claims from other offices along the coast. Mick worked at many other places in California. I'll bet we discover he's dated women at each of those offices, to gain access to their computers, to steal info to sell."

Roman's face was grim. "That would explain why he showed up here without Asia. He wants to get his hands on the data she sent, to cover his tracks and shut you up. He took a shot at you and more than likely overheard our conversation with Lloyd and killed him when he found out the guy was a P.I."

"Why not just let me take the blame instead? Or Asia?"

He shook his head. "He must have figured you'd put two and two together, or the cops would, so he needed to take care of anyone who could incriminate him."

Jackie's stomach convulsed. "But where is Asia? What has he done with her?"

Roman's brow furrowed. "We'll go to the police. They'll contact SFPD and start looking for her."

She heard a noise from outside as the man fired the engine of his snowmobile and drove away. A rumble of memory shot through Jackie's mind. The terror in Asia's voice when she'd called. And a strange sound Jackie had only just that moment identified. Horror seized her and she shot to her feet. "She's here. Asia is here in Alaska. I think Mick has got her at his cabin."

TWENTY-FIVE

Roman ran to the back office to find Wayne. Jackie yelled over his shoulder, "I heard a sound in the background when she called. I didn't realize it at first, but it was a snowmobile engine. He must have her, that's why he was so desperate to keep Fallon away when she showed up asking him for a ride, and why he didn't want to spend the night at Delucchi's during the blizzard."

Wayne listened to the tale, his eyes wide. "You sure about this?"

Roman let out a breath and flicked a glance at Wayne. "There are too many coincidences. I think she's right."

"I'll phone it in to the police."

Jackie shook her head violently. "We can't wait for them. Asia's in trouble. We have to get to her now."

Wayne grabbed keys and a phone. "I'll call on the way. We'll put the snowmobiles in the back and go in the truck as far as we can."

Roman turned to Jackie. "You should stay here. Wait for the police."

"No. I'm going with you."

The stubborn jut of her chin and the glimmer in those amber eyes made him want to grab her and kiss her breathless. Instead he ran out into the falling snow and helped Wayne load two snowmobiles in the back of the truck.

Roman got behind the wheel, and Jackie and Wayne crammed in next to him. He pushed the vehicle onto the road as fast as he dared. "Call the lodge," he yelled over the roar of the engine. "Tell Dax our suspicions, in case Mick shows up there looking for you."

Jackie braced herself against his shoulder to counteract the jolting of the truck. "Why would Mick concoct this whole business about Asia flying in today, anyway? What was he going to do when she didn't show up?"

He risked a quick look at her. "I think he was getting desperate after he murdered Lloyd. He intended to get the thumb drive from you and then…"

She gave him a look filled with such fear it made his breath catch.

"Then…he was going to kill me?"

He took her hand and squeezed it. "No one is going to hurt you. I promise you that." At that moment he felt a need stir inside him, stronger than it had in their carefree past, mightier than the power of the guilt that had consumed him. He wanted more than anything to tell her what was in his heart, but it was not the time.

Help me, Lord. Help me see this through for Jackie.

And for myself.

He kept the truck on the main road as long as he could. The road was snow-covered, but still passable. A deep gorge ran along one side of the paved surface. When they reached the winding path to the hunting cabin, he pulled off on the shoulder.

Roman got on one snowmobile and Jackie hopped on the other before Wayne could.

Wayne watched Jackie, then shot Roman an exasperated look. "She's as stubborn as you are."

He smiled. "I know. Direct the police up, and a rescue crew if they send one. I'll call you if we run into trouble."

Wayne's face was grave. "Be careful. This guy's murdered once, and he doesn't have a lot to lose."

Jackie had already started up the slope. He pressed the gas and shot through the falling snow after her.

I've got to get to Asia. The thought pounded through Jackie's mind like a relentless curtain of hail. Her friend was alive, but Mick must have her tied up or something. She wondered how he had managed to get her to the cabin in the first place. Jackie's own gullibility stabbed at her.

How could I have been tricked so easily?

The fear had been so real—Mick's beating, the stranger asking about her family, the confrontation with Dr. Reynolds, the threatening messages. It was all lies and misunderstandings, but it had been enough to send her on the run, leaving her job and security behind.

I ran away from everything I love.

Not everything, she thought with a start, watching Roman's strong shoulders as he guided the snowmobile upslope. The reality crept across her consciousness. There was something at work here bigger than the choices she'd made, the clues she hadn't seen. In fleeing San Francisco, she'd run right into the life God intended for her, the life she'd turned away from because of anger and hurt. In the face of the mounting fear, she felt a peace that she hadn't known since before Danny died.

She was here in Alaska because she belonged here, with Roman. Her heart warmed in spite of the freezing snowfall. They were meant to be together, but would he ever allow it? Could he forgive himself for Danny's death and let them have a future again? Would he allow himself to feel the love he'd known before?

The uncertainty added even more worry to her heavy heart, so she tried to concentrate on the task at hand. The snow-covered roof of the hunting cabin appeared at the top of the ridge. Roman signaled her to stop a hundred yards from it and they pulled their snowmobiles behind the concealing branches of a cluster of pines.

He took binoculars from the compartment on the back of the vehicle and scanned the horizon.

"No sign of Mick. His snowmobile's gone. He probably went looking for you in town."

She suppressed a shiver. "Any lights?"

He shook his head. "No, and we've got to get moving before the storm kicks up. He may have moved her to another location or…" Roman looked at her uneasily. "Are you sure you won't stay here?"

"I'm sure."

"Okay." He handed her a crowbar he took from the snow-mobile. "Keep this close. If there's trouble, get back to the truck and tell Wayne to get you out of here."

"I'm not leaving you."

His mouth tightened. "Yes, you are."

"Roman." She was filled with all the things she wanted to say, the feelings she wanted to share, but she could not give voice to the words. "I'm staying."

He sighed and they moved upslope, keeping to the cover of the trees as much as they could.

Her feet sank into the snow up to her shins with every step. The cold grabbed hold and penetrated deep inside. As they struggled toward the cabin, her fear increased. She heard again the shot that could have taken her life, whistling through the air. The motion of a bird in the branches made her heart hammer.

Was he out there? Waiting for the perfect shot? She struggled to keep up. When she foundered in a pocket of loose snow, she almost screamed aloud until Roman pulled her free. He held her close for a moment.

"Okay?"

She gritted her teeth and nodded. As much as she wanted to stay in the shelter of his arms, she knew they had more pressing business. He released her and they plowed on, until they were within yards of the quiet cabin.

Roman held a finger to his lips and tiptoed to a side window to peer in. Jackie joined him, too short to see over the sill.

"Is she in there?"

"Not in the kitchen or front room," he whispered. "Let's go around the back."

They crept around the perimeter of the wood-sided cabin, until they reached the porch. The darkness made it impossible to see much of anything in the interior except a small living area that opened onto a back hallway. There was no sign of Asia.

Roman tried the back door and found it locked. He gestured for the crowbar and smashed a hole in the window, just above the door handle.

The sound of breaking glass sounded loud in the stillness. Jackie held her breath and waited for the sound of running feet. They crouched low on either side of the door so they would not be visible.

Minutes ticked by. Nothing. No one stirred inside the cabin.

Jackie's panic swelled. Had she been completely wrong about Mick? Her mind was such a muddle of betrayals and half truths she did not trust her own powers of reasoning. She wondered if they should go back and wait for the police.

But if there was a chance, the smallest possibility that Asia was inside and needed help, she would not turn away. She locked eyes with Roman and nodded.

He reached a hand through the hole and unlocked the door. It swung open into the dark, silent space.

* * *

Roman wished more than ever that Jackie had stayed with Wayne in the truck. If they were wrong about Mick, he would be the only one guilty of breaking and entering. If they were right, Mick might arrive at any moment. He stepped into the kitchen, avoiding the broken glass that littered the floor. A half-eaten loaf of bread, a jar of peanut butter and a bag of chips on the counter confirmed that Mick had been in the hunting cabin recently.

The kitchen led into a small living room. Aside from a rumpled blanket and the lingering scent of burned wood from the fireplace, there was no sign of anyone. For the first time Roman noticed how cold it was in the cabin. A narrow hallway led to the back of the house where he knew the bedroom would be.

Making sure Jackie was behind him, he eased down the hallway. There were no windows to let in any light. The wood floor squeaked under his weight. They passed a tiny bathroom with a razor and assortment of shampoos and toothpaste.

Finally they reached a closed door, which Roman knew led to the bedroom. He eased the cold handle. The door was locked.

Jackie shot him a desperate look. "Should I call out?" she whispered.

Roman shook his head. "Might be a trap."

She bit her lip.

Roman pulled her back down to the end of the hallway and whispered in her ear. "I'm going to break it down. Get ready to run if you need to."

She grabbed his arm. "But if he's in there, with the rifle…"

He pulled her close and kissed her, hoping she could feel the emotion on his lips. Then he let her go and sprinted down the hallway, kicking at the locked door with all his strength.

TWENTY-SIX

The door exploded inward with the deafening sound of splintering wood. Jackie followed Roman into the room, her heart in her throat. It took a moment for her eyes to adjust to the dark, since the curtains were pulled securely over the windows.

She blinked, willing her eyes to take it all in.

But there was nothing to see.

Only a neatly made bed and a small lamp perched on a bedside table.

Jackie groaned. "She's not here. I was wrong. Oh, Roman, I was wrong."

Roman didn't answer. He walked to the bedside table and retrieved a bottle concealed in the shadow of the lamp. He held it out to her. "Sleeping pills."

"Pills? Why…?"

He held up a hand and began to slowly walk the perimeter of the room. "Sometimes people put in hidden rooms, to store their gun collections or extra food in case of bad weather." He stopped when his fingers found a rectangular outline in the wood-paneled wall. Reaching down to the bottom where the wall met the floor, he found a small indentation that served as a handle, all but invisible to the casual observer.

He motioned her away, and pulled it open.

A minute later he stepped inside. "Jackie, come here."

His voice was intense, but she needed no urging. She was in the tiny room in a flash.

The space was no bigger than a walk-in closet, the far wall lined with a gun rack filled with rifles. On a small cot lay her friend.

"Asia, can you hear me?" Jackie sank down and grabbed her cold hand. The girl didn't answer. "She's freezing."

He nodded, pulling the thin wool blanket around her body. "No heat. Only the blanket to keep her warm."

They chafed at her wrists until her eyes fluttered open.

"Jackie?" she whispered. "How did you find me? I thought…" Tears collected in her dark eyes and ran down her haggard face. "I thought I would die here."

Jackie squeezed her fingers. "No, honey. No. It's going to be okay."

Asia shuddered suddenly. "It's him. It's Mick."

Jackie tried to calm her. "I know. We figured it out."

Tears trickled down her face. "I thought he loved me. I really believed him. He was using me, like he used all the other girls at the other offices."

Jackie wiped her face. "You don't have to talk about it now. We'll work it all out."

She shook her head, eyes pained. "I just didn't see it. Maybe I didn't want to. Mick tried to discourage me from investigating the discrepancies I found. I thought he was worried about my safety. Dumb, huh?"

"I believed him too."

"Then when he showed up with a black eye and broken ribs." Her eyes closed. "At least, he told me they were broken, but that was a lie too. I'm not sure he even knows when he's lying. He's crazy. He idolized his father but when his dad and mom got divorced, everything fell apart for him."

Jackie remembered the look in Mick's eyes when he spoke about his father.

"His brother overcame, became a surgeon and Mick just couldn't stand it. He wanted to be somebody important, somebody with money and power." She sighed. "I think he might have fallen in with the crime ring when he worked at his brother's medical office. Remember, he told us about a crooked doctor there?"

Jackie nodded.

"I'm sure he didn't want to tell his boss about how we were looking into Reynolds's billing practices because it made Mick look like he'd been careless."

Jackie shook her head. "I can't believe you were here all the time, Asia. Why didn't you go to the police in San Francisco when you figured out it was Mick?"

She grimaced. "I didn't put it together until we landed in Alaska. That's when I heard him on the phone. He told whoever it was he'd 'clean it all up.' Suddenly the pieces fell together, but it was too late. He brought me here. I didn't see a single soul to ask for help."

Roman patted her shoulder. "That's the downside of living in remote Alaska. You can go a long time without running into any neighbors."

She nodded, sniffling. "I got hold of my phone for a minute, when he wasn't paying attention, but he found me and took it away. Oh, Jackie, I'm so sorry. I've been such a fool and it almost got us both killed. We should have gone straight to the police, the minute I had a suspicion."

Jackie took both her hands. "We were tricked, both of us, by a man who is as good a liar as anyone I've ever met."

Roman tapped his watch. "Asia, if you think you can move, we need to get out of here. It's going to be dark soon, and we'd better get you to the hospital and let the police handle things when Mick returns."

Jackie helped Asia to a sitting position and pulled on her shoes. She was cold, so cold and thin.

She felt suddenly furious. "Did he feed you? Please tell me he did that much."

Asia nodded. "Yes. And he brought me a blanket and let me out to use the bathroom, but other than that, I've been trapped in here. I begged him—I told him I'd never tell a soul." She began to shiver uncontrollably, tears rolling down her face and soaking her shirt front.

Jackie squeezed her in a hug. "Don't think about it right now. We'll get through this as soon as you're someplace safe. Okay?"

Asia pressed her lips together and stood on shaky legs.

Jackie tucked an arm under her shoulder and steadied her friend while Roman found her jacket in the bedroom closet and bundled her in. They made their way through the quiet cabin, stopping to listen every few feet for the sound of Mick's snowmobile returning.

Roman looked out the window into the swirling snow. "No sign of him."

He dialed Wayne's phone and told him they were returning with Asia.

"Right. No sign of our man down here. Cops are on their way."

Roman pocketed the phone and turned to both women. "Asia, we've got two snowmobiles and a truck parked about two miles downslope. Can you hold on to Jackie, just until we make it to the truck?"

Asia nodded, still shivering. "To get out of here, I can do anything."

He looked at Jackie.

She was overwhelmed once again. Here he was, putting everything on the line to help a woman he hardly knew.

Without warning, he leaned close and kissed her gently on the mouth. "Almost there."

She let the feeling linger on her skin.

And then they plunged into the snow.

Roman drove the lead snowmobile down the slope. They would be safe in another mile, back in the truck and headed to town. An inexplicable anxiety nestled in his gut. Something felt off. Paranoia? Fear that he'd lose Jackie now, when she had become his entire world again?

He tried to focus on the gleaming piles of snow that collected on the road, picking the smoothest route he could. Asia was probably near hypothermia and the shock of being out in the rapidly dropping temperature could push her over the edge.

They rounded a tree-lined bend in the road. He saw the truck, lit by the last rays of sunlight, and Wayne, hands tucked in pockets, waiting to greet them. He hustled over, his breath making puffs of silver in the near dark.

Wayne offered Asia a hand and helped her off. "You must be Asia. All right, ma'am?"

"Yes, but cold."

Roman didn't like the faintness of her voice. She was getting weaker. "Let's move."

Jackie helped Wayne load Asia up in the cab of the truck. Roman quickly slid the machines into the back and climbed up behind them. "Okay, Wayne. We're…"

His voice was lost in the rifle shot.

It drilled through the front windshield, splintering the glass into a web of cracks.

"Get down," he yelled, leaping off the truck and scrambling to the front.

Wayne was bleeding from a cut on his head. "When I get hold of that guy, he's paying for this windshield."

With relief, he turned to Jackie where she crouched over Asia, shielding her.

"I'm okay." She swallowed hard. "Asia is too. Is it Mick?"

"I think so. He must have circled around in front." Another shot exploded over them, burying itself into a tree and showering snow on them.

"We're pinned down. I'm going up to get him."

Jackie grabbed his arm, her fingers digging into his forearm. "No, he'll kill you."

He covered her hand with his own. "I'm not going to let him kill me. I've got something important to do." He gave her a tight smile, hating the fear that shone in her eyes.

"Let's wait for the police. Please, Roman."

"We might not have that much time. Keep Asia safe."

He ignored her cry of protest and called to Wayne. "As soon as the shooting stops, get this truck out of here. Don't wait for me."

Wayne gave him a long look and nodded. "Careful, son."

Careful. As Roman crept into the trees, using the truck for cover, he knew he'd have to be as careful as he'd ever been in his life.

The shots came from behind an outcropping of rock, off to the right side of the road. The spot was accessible by a steep trail, nestled among massive alder and pines. Roman's mind raced as he made his way closer.

They were locked in a waiting game, and Mick could not afford it to go on much longer. He could get off several shots from his position, but he could not be certain he'd done the job. He would need to move closer—Roman was counting on it.

He had to know they had phones, had probably called the police, so he'd be in a hurry to finish things and get away, hide until he could find an escape route. Yes, Mick would be in a hurry.

Roman smiled. If there was one thing Alaskans knew about, it was patience.

He found the perfect tree, just below the bend in the road, and began to climb.

TWENTY-SEVEN

Roman climbed in swift silence as he had countless times in his wild Alaska childhood. He tried to dislodge as little snow as possible, shimmying out onto a sturdy branch that thrust slightly over the path below. A cloud drifted in front of the moon, leaving the branches cloaked in darkness. He allowed a moment for his eyes to adjust before he laid stomach down on the tree bough.

The early night was silent, except for the brush of wind against the snow and the faraway cry of a wolf. He quieted his breathing to hear the tiniest sound that might give away Mick's intent. A boreal owl, disturbed by Roman's presence, fluttered to a lower branch, eyeing him warily.

Roman didn't have to wait long. The crunch of snow from the outcropping was followed by the hiss of a body sliding down the rock. After a moment Mick appeared, dressed in black, a knit cap pulled over his head. He held the rifle tight to his body and began the climb down the path.

Roman watched him pick his way along. He'd have no reason to look up, wouldn't even think about it, most likely. Roman eased one leg down over the side of the branch as Mick drew closer. He could see the white of his eyes, as he looked nervously up and down the path. Muscles tensed, he waited for Mick to come alongside the tree.

Just a few more feet, Mick. And it will be over before you know what hit you.

Jackie comforted the weeping Asia as much as she could.

"It's okay. It's going to be okay. The police are on their way."

Jackie's words did not ease her own state of terror. She looked at Wayne, who held a blood-soaked cloth to his head and a phone to the opposite ear. "Why did the shooting stop? What's happening?"

"Could be he needed to reload. Or Roman got him." He listened into the phone. "Police are ten minutes out."

"Roman never should have gone out there alone." She put a hand on the truck door. "I'm going to help him."

Wayne held up a hand. "The only thing you'll accomplish climbing up there is giving Roman's plan away."

"There's got to be something."

His gaze was stern. "Do you know those woods?"

She scanned the dark, wooded slope. She might have, once upon a time, but now, in the dark, she knew she would be lost in a matter of minutes. The what-ifs thundered through her brain.

Mick was determined and ruthless. He'd used Asia without a shred of guilt or regret. He'd killed Byron Lloyd to cover his own tracks. He would not hesitate for a moment to kill Roman too.

Her heart hammered inside her chest, almost drowning out Wayne.

He gripped her arm. "Roman's smart, he's tough and he knows the terrain. Mick hasn't got a chance."

She nodded, willing the words to kindle a surge of hope inside. She felt only numbing fear. The snow fell in a steady curtain, swallowing them in a soundless basket.

Asia leaned against her shoulder, crying softly. Jackie tried again to chafe her shoulders, but she could not warm her friend enough to stop the shivers. The Delucchi Lodge, town, Wayne's shuttle business, it all seemed a million miles away. There was only darkness in every direction.

Roman eased his weight forward as Mick came closer. The man moved warily, placing each booted foot down into the snow with precision. He stopped to wipe the flakes from his eyes and the sweat from his forehead. Then he continued on, step after step until he was only two feet from Roman's hiding place.

Come on, come on. It was time to end this mess, to give Jackie her life back. For a brief moment, he wondered if he could share in that life, if there was any way God could put the pieces back together for them.

There's only one way, Roman. And you know what you need to do.

Mick was so close now Roman could see the ice crystals that clung to his eyebrows. Five more steps, three, then two.

Mick stepped on a slick patch of ice and skidded. Convulsively, he gripped the rifle, and the movement frightened the owl. The animal flapped its thick wings, creating just enough movement to catch Mick's eye. Instinctively, Mick fired off a shot as he looked up.

The shot split the silence. Jackie screamed.

She stared at Wayne, hands halfway to her mouth, balled into fists.

He took a slow breath. "Don't jump to conclusions. We don't know what happened."

"Roman would never have shot Mick unless he had to." Her voice sounded shrill and tinny to her own ears, as if her words were spoken by someone else.

He straightened. "I see the police lights about two miles down. They'll be here soon."

Her body took over. She wrenched open the door and jumped out.

"No, Jackie. Stay here."

Wayne's voice faded into the distance as she ran up the slope, stumbling over snow-covered rocks and sinking knee-deep in loose snow.

Roman, Roman, Roman.

Mick turned his face upward, with just enough time for his eyes to widen in shock before Roman hurtled from the tree. They fell in a tangle of limbs and skidded several yards downslope.

Roman grabbed the end of the rifle with one hand and Mick's arm with the other.

Mick struggled to get his footing and throw off his attacker.

They continued to slide until they crashed into the rocks at the edge of the road where it fell off into a steep hollow. Mick slammed the rifle butt into Roman's ribs, setting off a shower of pain. Roman managed to knee Mick in the stomach, pushing him away long enough to scramble to his feet.

Mick did the same, backing to the edge of the road, eyes wild, readying the rifle.

They stood there panting, the moon painting them the same shadowed color as the snowy woods around them.

Mick aimed the gun at Roman's heart. "If it isn't the Wilderness Boy."

Roman did not feel afraid as he looked at Mick. "You don't get it do you? You're in Alaska. You can't just run home. The only way in or out is to fly, and you'll never get on a plane without being caught. The police are on their way now. You're done."

Mick snarled. "I've survived this long and I'll manage."

Roman laughed. "That's what all the city slickers say. This is Alaska, Mick. You can't beat Alaska."

"Watch me." Mick took a step back, finger on the trigger.

It was one step too many. The loose snow along the edge of the road gave way and he tumbled backwards, the rifle dropping harmlessly on the snow. Roman ran to the edge and watched Mick pinwheel into a pile at the bottom of the hollow. After a second or two he tried to scramble up, but he must have broken his ankle in the fall and he sank back down with a howl of pain.

Roman smiled down at him as the sirens drew close. "I'll tell the other wilderness boys where to find you," he called down.

City slicker.

He turned at a sound and then Jackie was in his arms, crying, laughing, unable to speak. He cupped her lovely face in his cold hands.

"I'm surprised you held out so long before you came charging up here."

She laughed. "And I'm surprised it took you so long to take Mick down."

He shrugged. "Must be from hanging around with you West Coast-types."

She raised her eyes to his. "You know what? Deep down inside, I think I've always been an Alaskan."

He traced the line of her tears with his finger. "You know what? I think you're right."

He found her lips with his.

The police arrived and sent two men down to strap Mick to a stretcher and haul him out. Jackie and Roman waited there until Mick was secured and then walked back to the truck.

Wayne clapped Roman on the back. "Knew you'd get him."

"He got himself, really. Where's Asia?"

"Couple of cops took her ahead to the hospital. They said to meet them there."

Roman raised an eyebrow. "And why didn't you go with them and get your wound looked at?"

Wayne turned away and reached for his keys. "Just a scratch. Let's go."

"Sure, but I'm driving."

Roman eased the truck onto the road and drove slowly back to town, where he dropped his friend back at Wayne's Aviation. He knew it was useless to try to talk him into being checked out by a doctor.

Wayne leaned in the window and gave Jackie a kiss on the cheek. "Don't keep him out too late. He's got a ten o'clock flight to do for me tomorrow."

Jackie laughed. "I'll do my best."

They drove toward the hospital, sitting close together to try to fend off the chill caused by the hole in the front windshield. Roman started to speak, but the words refused to leave his mouth.

He coughed and tried again with no better result.

She reached over and took his hand.

He watched the wipers gently clear the snow from the windshield and it seemed to mirror what was happening in his soul. He tried again. "Jackie, I want you to know how sorry I am about Danny. If I could have one moment, one second to do it all over again, I would. For years I wished it was me that had died in that accident and not your brother."

She squeezed his fingers. "Roman…"

"Let me finish. Please." He pulled the truck into the hospital parking lot and turned off the motor. "Something changed when you came back. I'm not sure why, but somehow it seemed like maybe we could put that behind us, like you'd forgiven me." He shot her a quick look. "Did I get things right? Or am I seeing what I want to see?"

Her eyes filled. "Roman, I do forgive you. It was a terrible accident, that's all, and I was wrong to hold that anger in for so long. I refused to forgive you and I'm sorry for that."

He shook his head. "No, I didn't want to be forgiven, really. I wanted to keep that pain alive to punish myself for what I'd done. But I think…"

She stroked his palm with her warm fingers. "Tell me."

"I think I need to ask God to forgive me, and allow myself to accept it."

She nodded and bowed her head.

"Heavenly Father…" Roman began.

Jackie walked into the hospital feeling as if a full ton of weight had been lifted off her shoulders. She could tell by the subtle straightening of Roman's back, and the way he cradled her arm in his, that he felt the same way too. It had taken years of grief and anger and pain, but they'd made it, embracing God's precious gift of forgiveness. He'd given them back their lives.

But what would the future look like? She wasn't certain. Though she felt on the deepest level of her soul that she wanted to stay in Alaska, to make a home there, she knew she would not, unless he asked her.

They walked to the reception desk and a state trooper met them.

He nodded. "Looks like your friend will be fine. She's lucky. You're all lucky. We got a full confession from Mick."

Jackie sagged in relief. "I can't believe it's over."

"We still need to talk to you about the details. For now, I'll take the thumb drive. We'll need it and the cooperation of Dr. Reynolds to piece all this together."

She started. "I forgot all about that. I left it with Wayne."

Roman wrapped an arm around Jackie and smiled at the

trooper. "Well, if you need any expertise, Wayne is pretty up on the particulars."

The trooper looked at him and grinned. "He's got the investigation bug going on, huh?"

"Yeah. He's got it bad."

The officer laughed. "I'll look him up, all right." He shook his head. "Financial stuff is going to be like reading Greek to me."

They gave the officer their phone numbers and he left.

Jackie was surprised to see Fallon coming toward them, her hair pulled back in a ponytail.

"Hey. Why are you guys here?"

Jackie looked at Roman, who raised an eyebrow and sighed.

"It's a really long story." He shook his head. "I'll fill you in soon, I promise. How is your mother?"

Fallon shrugged. "Okay. Want to go see her? I'm tired of trying to make conversation."

They followed her to the elevator and up two flights. The door of June's room was open, the space softly illuminated, in contrast to the darkened hallway. As they approached, Skip stepped into the doorway, lit from behind.

Jackie almost plowed into Roman as he stopped dead. "Roman?"

He stood frozen, staring at Skip, his eyes wide, mouth open in surprise.

Her stomach clenched. "What is it? What's wrong?"

Roman opened his mouth but did not speak. Finally, he whispered, "It was you."

Skip stepped out into the hallway. "What's that?"

"All this time, I've tried to remember, and now I have, right now. It was you."

"I don't know what you're talking about. Come and sit down." He walked toward them but Roman jerked back.

Jackie came close to him and put her hand on his back. She

could feel his heart jackhammering inside his chest. "What did you remember?"

Roman closed his eyes. "That night, the night Danny died. I drove us around the bend and suddenly there was a vehicle there, going fast in the other direction. I slammed on the brakes and we skidded off the side of the road. After we crashed I had just a glimpse of someone standing there, watching." He turned blazing eyes on Skip. "It was you. Your snowmobile almost hit us and you stood there and watched us after the crash."

Jackie went numb with shock. "What? That can't be true. Tell me that isn't true, Skip."

Fallon's face was white as paste. She stared at her father. "I think it is true. I asked Danny to go into town to find out the truth for me, and you must have heard. You heard and you wanted to stop him so you went to the cabin." Her voice dropped to a whisper. "That's what happened, isn't it?"

Jackie fought to put the information into some sort of sane order. "Find out what? Fallon, what did you ask my brother to do?"

Skip cleared his throat. "She asked Danny to find her birth mother."

The silence was complete.

Finally, Roman spoke in a voice no louder than a murmur. "The woman in the picture. The lady who worked for you when you were building this place. She's Fallon's mother."

Skip nodded, face slack with emotion. "She was pregnant and didn't want the baby. She gave her to us and left. Set up a life in Arizona. Then several years ago, she started contacting us for money, blackmailing us that if she didn't get what she asked for, she'd come back for Fallon."

Tears streamed down the girl's cheeks. "Why didn't you tell me? Why did you lie to me about her?"

"We kept putting it off when you were little and then when

you grew up we were afraid that you'd leave." His voice broke. "We were afraid."

Roman laughed, a harsh, biting noise. "Afraid? Is that why you left Danny and me there after the accident? You were afraid? Is that why you refused to tell the truth about your part in it all this time?"

Skip bowed his head. "I didn't intend for the accident to happen. I was going to make up some excuse, some lie to get Danny off the idea. I didn't think it through. After the crash, I was in shock. I didn't know what to do. I called for help, I tried to get down to the crash but it was too steep so I…"

"Drove away." Roman's words were bitter. "And left Danny to die."

Skip began to tremble. "If I could have helped, I would have. I panicked. I never meant to hurt him. Or you."

Jackie heard Fallon's anguished sob.

Skip let out a low moan and sank to his knees. "I'm sorry, Roman. Jackie. I'm so sorry."

Jackie felt the anger and shock drain out of her at the sight of him on the floor. What he'd done, or hadn't, wouldn't bring her brother back, and there had been enough blame surrounding her brother's death to last a lifetime. The only thing she could think about was Roman, all those years suffering under a lie from someone he'd trusted. She wanted it all to be over, but she knew it was not her forgiveness he needed.

Roman was completely still except for the quick rise and fall of his chest.

"I've been sorry every day, every moment," Skip whispered. "I loved Danny like a son, and you too, Roman. I can't believe I let things turn out this way."

"You let me live with what happened for two years."

Tears rolled down his face. "Yes. I don't deserve your pity or forgiveness. I'm sorry. I'm so sorry."

After what seemed like a lifetime, Roman spoke, almost painfully. "It's not the time for this. Fallon and June need you now."

The look Skip shot him was filled with pain. He lifted his hands, fingers trembling. "Roman, can you ever…?"

Roman cleared his throat. "It's going to take some time, for all of us." Then, ever so slowly, he reached forward and held a hand out to Skip. They didn't say a word. Skip clung to him as Roman helped him up, and stayed there, his fingers gripped tight until the knuckles whitened.

Fallon's mouth was open. Roman took her fingers in his free hand. "This is going to hurt, but your father did wrong for the right reasons. He loves you and your mother. You've got to remember that."

Fallon hunched over as if she felt a pain her stomach, then she hurled herself into her father's arms, almost knocking him over. "Daddy."

"I'm sorry, baby. I love you so much. I'm going to make up for what I've done. I'll go talk to the police. I'll make it right for you and your mom. And Roman."

Skip gave Roman and Jackie a final anguished look before he walked into June's room, Fallon clutching him around the waist.

Jackie turned Roman to face her, her own face damp with tears. "Why did you do that?"

He sighed. "I didn't do anything."

"You could have cut him down, raged at him for what he's done. It would have been completely understandable, but you didn't."

"I'm not sure I understand it myself. I'm angry at what he did to Danny, and how he let me suffer alone."

Jackie stayed silent, watching the bemused expression on his face, unsure how she felt about Skip's revelation. She should have been angry at Skip, furious, but for some reason all she could think about was Roman.

He locked eyes on hers. "I think I realized how guilt has kept me away from the person I love most in the world, and I don't want to heap that on anyone else. Forgiving Skip won't be easy, but I'm going to try to work at it."

"Me too." She felt the tears well up. "I love you too, Roman. I don't think I ever really stopped."

"I love you too." He embraced her and kissed her hair. "I'm going to buy that plane someday and build a company here. I can make a good life, a future for the both of us."

She cupped his cheek in her palm and allowed herself to feel the joy she'd never thought she'd experience again. "We can make a good life together."

He kissed her again with exquisite tenderness.

The warmth filled her up, driving out the last of the shadows from her soul.

* * * * *

Dear Reader,

> Though your sins are as scarlet,
> They will be as white as snow:
> Though they are red like crimson,
> They will be like wool.
>
> Isaiah 1:18

We know it's true that the Lord forgives our sins, that He sent His Son to wash us white as snow. Why, then, is it so hard to walk away from our past mistakes and hurts? Or to extend forgiveness to others who have hurt us deeply? Jackie Swann must learn to forgive Roman Carter, the man she blames for taking her brother's life. For his part, Roman struggles to believe himself worthy of any forgiveness, heavenly or otherwise. When Jackie's survival hinges on the man she's sworn to shun forever, she and Roman must open their hearts to God's abundant grace in order to make it through a deadly Alaska winter.

I humbly thank you, dear reader, for spending time with this story. Alaska is a vast country filled with wonder and wilderness. I hope you will enjoy journeying along with Jackie and Roman through this pristine place. It is always a thrill to hear from readers. I invite you to send any comments or questions via my Web site, www.danamentink.com.

Fondly,

Dana Mentink

QUESTIONS FOR DISCUSSION

1. Jackie makes a decision in the first chapter that changes the rest of her life. Have you ever made a split-second decision that had long-lasting consequences?

2. Alaskan bush pilots see some of the most beautiful, rugged terrain on the planet. What kind of personality traits would be necessary to be successful in this job?

3. The Delucchi Lodge holds memories both sweet and painful for Jackie. How would things be different for her if she had stayed in Alaska after her brother's death?

4. Did Jackie's father make the right decision, leaving Alaska forever after Danny died?

5. Do you think Roman made the right choice to stay in Alaska after Danny's death?

6. If you traveled to a remote location, which piece of technology would you miss the most?

7. The Delucchi Lodge provides guests with almost total isolation from the frantic pace of the Lower 48. Would you be happy in such a place? Why or why not?

8. Jackie's father encourages her feelings of anger toward Roman. Have you experienced pressure from a loved one to hold a grudge and hold on to past hurts?

9. The northern lights draw people from all over the world. In our age of high-tech wizardry, why does this natural display continue to fascinate the masses?

10. Have you felt reluctant to ask for forgiveness? Is it a sin to hold onto guilt instead of accepting His divine gift of grace?

11. The Delucchis made a desperate effort to keep the truth from Fallon. In your view, how could they have handled the situation differently?

12. Alaska is a remote place. Do you think you would be able to live in a place like that? Why or why not?

13. How do you think the limited amount of sunlight in Alaska affected the characters?

14. What do you think Jackie will do for a career in Alaska, now that she's going to live there?

15. How do you think you would react if you were caught in an avalanche like Jackie and Roman were?

*Scandal surrounds Rebecca Gunderson after she
shares a storm cellar during a deadly
tornado with Pete Benjamin.
No one believes the time she spent with
him was totally innocent.
Can Pete protect her reputation?*

*Read on for a sneak peek of
HEARTLAND WEDDING by Renee Ryan,
Book 2 in the AFTER THE STORM:
THE FOUNDING YEARS series
available February 2010
from Love Inspired Historical.*

"Marry me," Pete demanded, realizing his mistake as the words left his mouth. He hadn't asked her. He'd told her.

He tried to rectify his insensitive act but Rebecca was already speaking over him. "Why are you willing to spend the rest of your life married to a woman you hardly know?"

"Because it's the right thing to do," he said.

Angling her head, she caught her bottom lip between her teeth and then did something utterly remarkable. She smoothed her fingertips across his forehead. "As sweet as I think your gesture is, you don't have to save me."

A pleasant warmth settled over him at her touch, leaving him oddly disoriented. "Yes, I do."

She dropped her hand to her side. "I don't mind what others say about me. You and I, *we,* know the truth."

Pete caught her hand in his, and turned it over in his palm. "I told Matilda Johnson we were getting married."

She snatched her hand free. "You…you…*what?*"

He spoke more slowly this time. "I told her we were getting married."

She did *not* like his answer. That much was made clear by her scowl. "You shouldn't have done that."

"She was blaming you for luring me into my own storm cellar."

The color leached out of Rebecca's cheeks as she sank into a nearby chair. "I…I simply don't know what to say."

"Say yes. Mrs. Johnson is a bully. Our marriage will silence her. I'll speak with the pastor today and—"

"No."

"—schedule the ceremony at once." His words came to a halt. "What did you say?"

"I said, no." She rose cautiously, her palms flat on her thighs as though to brace herself. "I won't marry you."

"You're turning me down? After everything that's happened today?"

"No. I mean, *yes.* I'm turning you down."

"Your reputation—"

"Is my concern, not yours."

She sniffed, rather loudly, but she didn't give in to her emotions. Oh, she blinked. And blinked. And *blinked.* But no tears spilled from her eyes.

Pete pulled in a hard breath. He'd never been more baffled by a woman. "We were both in my storm cellar," he reminded her through a painfully tight jaw. "That means we share the burden of the consequences equally."

Blink, blink, blink. "My decision is final."

"So is mine. We'll be married by the end of the day."

Her breathing quickened to short, hard pants. And then…*at last*…it happened. One lone tear slipped from her eye.

"Rebecca, please," he whispered, knowing his soft manner came too late.

"No." She wrapped her dignity around her like a coat of iron-clad armor. "We have nothing more to say to each other."

Just as another tear plopped onto the toe of her shoe, she turned and rushed out of the kitchen.

Stunned, Pete stared at the empty space she'd occupied. "That," he said to himself, "could have gone better."

Will Pete be able to change Rebecca's mind
and salvage her reputation?
Find out in HEARTLAND WEDDING
available in February 2010
only from Love Inspired Historical.

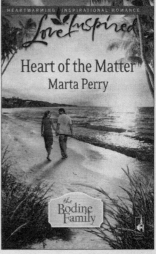